JOBEY

"Margaret, I'll take the job," he said flatly. He was never very articulate and now he felt overwhelmingly sad and quiet. She turned to him and they pressed close together, neither of them speaking; rather as if there had been a bitter argument which they had both lost.

"I want you to take it because *you* wanted to, Jobey. If you take it just to please me it will always come between us. You'll hate me when the men start to hate you; when they call you scab and blackleg; when the women beat pans and tins as you go by; when every friend you ever had hopes the roof is going to fall in on you. Your life will be empty, Jobey, and you will blame me, because I emptied it for you. I'll feel so guilty I'll want you to hate me. If anything happens to you, I'll hate myself. There's only me to take the place of all this, only me to fill the gap. What shall we do when the honeymoon's over? Oh, I don't know what's to become of us. Hold me close, Jobey, ever so close, so no-one can hurt us."

by the same author

The Crowded Cemetary

Death of a Portrait

took a shilling from his waistcoat pocket and slipped it on to the mantelpiece. It looked very bright amidst the dust and the red velvet cloth with bobbles hanging. The bobbles had been white once – in a time when Pop Rainbow had his *own* waistcoat full of shillings and walked with his back as straight as is possible for a miner.

Jobey did not miss the shillings just now. Doctor Alexander put a brand new sovereign in his hand every Friday night. A hard-earned gratis payment for "Assistance with the experiments". For many years now he had been a guinea-pig for the Doctor's unorthodox ideas on how to detect and combat gas in the pits, and for all his strength Jobey had nearly succumbed more than once.

He did not ask the owners how it was entered into expenses. The Waverley Bros., had a lot of expenses to bury, somehow, these days. Fighting the Federation was a dirty job and there was no quarter given or expected between owners and Federation officials. The tension was mounting daily now, but John Waverley was putting his faith in the Union body growing too big for its head. He had not been Chairman of the Company for fifteen years without learning something about men, fifteen difficult years from pre-war 1911 to this present Year of Grace, 1926.

Jobey went out without a word. He felt deeply about having to dole out his father's beer money in oddments, but he knew that if he gave too much at once there would be the job of collecting him from the sawdust covered floor of the "Dog and Fox". If this was not done before ten p.m. they were all treated to the spectacle of 'Killer' Calladine bringing Pop home in his wheelbarrow. "Killer' was a derisory title for a scarecrow of a man who had gravitated towards Pop because they had both been half-crippled by the same pit-pony. Common enemies making common friends. After a few pints Killer would impart a bit of confidential information to anyone within shouting distance. "There's me and another chap, ... we can fight any two men in Moorgreen," Killer then relapsed into a smug silence, ... that would set the buggers wondering!

Jobey had no time for such thoughts tonight. His footsteps were cushioned by a layer of coal dust as he passed along Engine Lane and over the crossings towards the open fields of

High Park where he was meeting Margaret. His heart was in his mouth and his huge muscles were nearly solid with tension. She was witty and gay, small, as precious things usually are. He felt oafish and inadequate, not in her league at all, but she had said she would meet him. His feeling of inferiority made him imagine the worst. Was she going to tease him, and relate what he said to her sophisticated friends? Must he be very formal and polite, so that everything he said would stand repeating? No, she wouldn't do that to him.

He swung along now by the reservoir in the late April sunshine. He looked down at the black patent leather shoes he had bought specially for this evening. They were so light he felt he could walk forever in them, not like the hard boots he wore every day when he walked this way six-hundred feet underground. He felt immensely fit and happy, to walk with head up and back erect and breathe in deeply the moist clean air and to have Margaret Booker as well – this night he must register every tiny impression, nothing must be lost or allowed to escape from his memory. He would hold her so close to him that if she never came again he could re-live the experience at any moment he wished. Under this water, where he spent most of his time down the pit, he could cross his arms, when no-one could see him, and squeeze, and remember, and be happy, and he wouldn't be down under this vast expanse of cold water at all. He would be with Margaret.

He looked towards Misk Hills and the trees which ran down to the water's edge. The setting sun made helter-skelter shadows which accentuated the steepness of the gullies. The sharp reflection of the trees undulated slowly here and there as the trout gently shook their blankets, making ready for night.

Jobey felt at home here, as if everything was thrusting down to reach his seam of coal. Sometimes when no-one was about at the coal face he put his hands on the roof to feel the weight of the trees and the water and to embrace all the good things that were above him. He entreated them to stay there and not encroach on the tiny bit that was his. There was no room to spare in that thin black slice of manna which fed the whole of Moorgreen. The two worlds were so close together and yet so far apart.

She was there already. Why had she come to meet him and not stayed at the gate as arranged? She didn't want Mr. Booker to know, that was it. There he was again, selling himself short. She was there, there, waiting for him, and his heart was so full of love he wanted to drop on one knee and thank her just for being there.

"Hello, Job". She looked up with those glistening eyes and he became aware of himself staring in frank admiration. She put her hand into his and tugged hard to get him going. He felt like a liner being moved from its berth, so cumbersome was his bulk.

"Hello, Margaret. Glad you came."

She looked down to where her hand was buried in his great calloused fists. He looked down also, but didn't let go. His searing love gave him courage and he pressed the palm to his lips. Her finger-tips touched his cheek and he knew his face was scarlet as the blood thumped into his ears. He had not intended to do this at all, but her presence overpowered him. He was so strung up with emotion he felt the tears coming into his eyes.

Margaret was not without experience; she decided he had better release the tension before something went bust inside him. She nestled into his arms and they kissed in the twilit country lane, and Jobey knew that if he lived to be a hundred he would never be this happy again.

"God, let the world stand still," he murmured. He touched the soft gold of her cheek with his finger-tips, cursing the hardness of his hands which dulled the sensitive texture. So this was a woman. He explored the roots of her hair with his eyes. He thumbed tenderly along the line of her eyebrows with thumbs which could crack a walnut. Effortlessly he picked her up to his level as if she were a doll, brushed her lips with his own, then very gently put her down.

"You quite finished, Job?" She smiled at him, and was obviously delighted.

He nodded dreamily, too happy to speak. He smiled sheepishly now that she brought him back to earth. As they went along he took very small steps, so that she did not have to hurry, but this put him off balance so that he went along like a three-legged horse.

"Job. Why do you let the Doctor experiment on you? What do you think will happen if he doesn't get the breathing apparatus on you quickly enough?"

"Everybody calls me Jobey, Margaret. It sounds more friendly somehow."

"Jobey, do you want to come to an early end? I'm surprised that Dr. Alexander manages to get you onto that contraption of a sledge down there."

"I try to collapse on it if I feel myself going. The Doctor knows what he's doing."

"If that were true he needn't experiment. What would you say if I asked you not to do it? For my sake? He's not a medical doctor you know. My father says he ought not to let you walk after you've been overcome by gas. It puts a strain on your heart, and anybody else would have died already."

Jobey kicked at a stone, and then remembered his patent shoes. He wondered if they were ruined but daren't look in case she realised it was the only pair he had. "He pays me for it, you know. And we travel all the old workings where nobody else is allowed. No-one knows more than we do, how to get about down there."

"So what? One dark tunnel is just like another. He'll get the pair of you killed. Do you know he's planning to burn chemicals down the pit next Sunday? Claims he can lower the oxygen content of the air so that no explosion can take place. You're going down there first, in case there's not enough oxygen left to support human life. They're even bringing the ponies up whilst he experiments. Only Jobey Rainbow will be down there. The men can think for themselves, so they get out. The ponies can't think for themselves, so they are brought out. I'd say that makes you part man, part horse. How much do they pay for a Centaur?"

Jobey was lost somewhere back with the oxygen bit, so he mumbled about being double pay for Sunday.

Margaret returned to the attack. "Dad says the Doctor's going off his head. I don't suppose he's told you that you two are deliberately going to make explosions down the pit to consume the gas. He is working on a contraption like a big candle holder on wheels, which you, Jobey, are going to work with long lengths of cord."

Jobey wanted to say that the only way he could ever get enough money together to ask Margaret to marry him was by taking these appalling risks with the Doctor.

"Sounds more like a job for 'Dobbin' than you." She kept up the attack.

Jobey smiled, "What do you know about *him*?" He was highly amused at first that she should ever have heard of Dobbin, but he didn't really want to pursue the subject. Dobbin was too much a part of Engine Lane and Jobey felt tainted by his knowledge of Dobbin and his ways.

One of Dobbin's pastimes was to sit outside the "Dog and Fox" on Saturday nights waiting for turning out time when he knew there would be a fight to watch. Somebody usually took pity on him and threw him the price of a pint and he shuffled inside, put his money on the bar and stood waiting, patient as a broody hen and with the same gormless expression. Jobey smiled faintly.

"You're thinking about Dobbin, aren't you?" Margaret laughed at Jobey's obvious discomfiture. "Penny for your thoughts Jobey Rainbow, come on, tell me about Dobbin."

Jobey writhed and looked at her out of the corner of his eye. Dobbin had been to the Goose Fair and had seen a fat lady in a side-show. The barker had pinched her in all sorts of unlikely places and kept calling out "Fat! Fat. It's all fat!" Dobbin had picked this up and went around calling "Fat! Fat. It's all fat." in a shrill voice like a parrot, his bird-like brain triggering the sentence off from time to time. "Better than the two-headed dog," Dobbin would drawl with a slow leer that showed he was aroused somewhere deep inside his wrinkled body.

Should he tell Margaret this? Should he tell her a dozen more things he knew about Dobbin? The depths of animal depravity the old man touched and which, Lord help him, amused them all. He was ashamed even to think of such things in her company. But he *was* Dobbin. The scent of the man was in his nostrils, the tales of the man were in his ears, and the weight of the knowledge of this pitiable heap of bones and flesh pinned him, Jobey Rainbow, down to Engine Lane; the long haul away from there to where Margaret lived seemed suddenly to be a lane without end. It was all a million miles away from Margaret Booker's world.

He had to have money. That was the key, that was what he must concentrate on.

He wanted to say that Engine Lane was no place for Margaret Booker, and without her he didn't care if he did get his brains blown out. What few he had. None of this could he say in reply, so he stared glumly at the two great hills on the other side of the reservoir. Joe Bird, the Union Secretary always said, "Jobey, better keep your mouth shut and be thought a fool, than to open it and remove all doubt."

Joe Bird could say all this for him. Jobey was his pet and loved it. To be able to talk like that, and have men cheering for you. Even Tater Varley cheered Joe Bird when he told them about sticking together. John Waverley and his brother Thomas were trying to break the Unions. Joe told them the Waverley Brothers had more money than all the miners put together. Here at Moorgreen in Nottinghamshire there were two thousand miners and only two brothers owned it. Jobey was all for Joe Bird, he spoke good sense and spoke it loud and clear. Even Jobey could understand him. He still felt important as he remembered Joe's words at the Lodge Meeting; "We've all got our parts to play before Nineteen twenty-six is out, but leave Jobey out of it, he is going to stick closer to me than a shadow,"

"Joe Bird knows all about it," Jobey said, by way of defence.

"Mr. Smart-Alec Bird."

Jobey, discomfited, kicked another stone, not a bit bothered about his shoes; it seemed unlikely that Margaret would notice such mundane objects.

"Mr. Bird should tell Dr. Alexander to stick to canaries for testing the oxygen," she said, then changed the conversation. She had said too much already, but she had to let him know how she felt. They appeared to be on opposite sides of the fence, well and truly.

"How's your Dad, Jobey?"

Jobey looked suddenly sad. Of course, she knew how things were. Everyone knew, even on Beauvale Drive, so, because he was completely without guile he simply said "Probably drunk by now."

She stopped and gave him a gentle kiss on the cheek. "Do you like it out here, Jobey? Look at the sheep still quietly feeding on those two round hills. What do they remind you of, Jobey?" She tried to raise his spirits.

"Like white maggots on a carcase." He was not to be consoled, and his strong body seemed to bend beneath the weight of his sudden depression. She drew his leathery hand to her cheek and he felt her tears run through his fingers. His eyes opened wide in surprise and he pulled her to him and held her tightly. He put his lips to her smooth perfect throat and breathed her into every fibre of his being, renewing his spirits.

"Oh Jobey!" she breathed. "What am I going to do about you?" She took his head into her hands and shook it good and hard, and fondled his ears, just as she did with her Great Dane. "Do you hear me? You have a head like a lion, Jobey." Her gentle lips brushed his ear. "You should live out here where God meant you to be. You could watch the hills through the changing seasons, have the sun on your face, frost on your ears. Men such as you belong in the open air."

He shook his head free and she could see the shadows in his eyes.

"That's where I belong." He pointed down at the water. "Under there, where a man doesn't have to know when to sit or stand, when to shake a hand or stand respectfully. We use the words our fathers taught us and ... and ..." The word Father was a ball and chain.

"And it's somewhere to hide," she interrupted. "It's dark and familiar, and you were born to it, I suppose." Now she had said her piece and they both stood quietly.

Margaret fixed her eyes on a tree which kept them company on this lonely hill. Stunted by the hill-top wind it had shed all but a top-knot of branches. It had a strong, weathered look, confident and unyielding, its roots had gone deep towards that underlying Mother-lode of coal which drew life to itself with a force that was stronger than gravity. Its roots went for the coal, with its slightly sweet smell of centuries-old forests, tinged with the sweat of labouring men, and the odour of ever-present death.

Jobey was a tree. That's what he was. His skin was hard

intractable bark. He was in his own domain and knew it. His roots were in coal and she was a fool to think otherwise. He was Engine Lane, big, hard, grimy, foreign to her upbringing. She shuddered.

"Let me go now, Jobey, I'm ready to go." In the fading light they walked back like two lovers who had drained themselves of all passion.

* * *

There were plenty of mundane things to occupy Jobey's mind. The miners' leaders were getting ready for war. A few shots had already been fired over the last six months. Germany had been paying reparations in coal to traditional British Markets, so overseas markets were drying up. Electricity was making great strides and there were bogies of some sort round every corner. It was a time of great depression. Ship-building, steel, engineering; the land fit for heroes was losing the peace. Coal prices struck an all-time low. The demand went down and down until miners' earnings were lower than engine cleaners', lower than almost any other industry in the land.

Basic problems such as desperately low wages could not be resolved overnight by an industry which was on its knees. If a head-on clash was not avoided now there would be no winners; only survivors. It was a time for talking, a time for giving as well as taking, but statesmen were lacking on both sides. They had to be culled from the heartache and deprivation of decent men, women and children, and they were a long time coming.

Every day the great heaps of coal grew higher. The sidings down Engine Lane, where Jobey lived, were solid with trucks full of coal. It was better for John Waverley than money in the bank, it was propaganda by the ton. Those who lived in its shadow could not fail to be impressed by the preparedness of the owners. It was a lot of coal, and when the miners compared it with their own slim resources in the Federation funds it was almost enough to put a man off his beer. But not quite.

In the "Dog and Fox" Tater Varley had the floor, as usual:

"Talking to a chap yesterday, reckons there's thousands of

Jerries being drafted into the pits if we strike."

"They'll be no good down Moorgreen, the spikes on their helmets 'll stick in the bloody roof." Sam Watson roared into his quart pot. His own jokes were always better than anybody else's. Sam was a bachelor so it was all right for him. It was common knowledge that he had a full book at the Co-op which meant two hundred pounds to his credit. He never fetched his Co-op "divi" when it was 'Moorgreen Races'. Moorgreen races was the day they paid out the divi, and queues formed at the little paying-out office.

That was usually a lean week for Rosie Button. Rosie was a pawnbroker's runner and took things for people who were too far up the social ladder to be seen in the shop. She kept ten per cent of what she got – and her secrets. When times got too lean Rosie ponched. She filled her great wooden tub and took in washing. Rosie was built like a Roman wall. Her husband had a weak chest, so she was bringing up five boys by her own efforts. She could eat two pigs' feet for breakfast with a saucerful of pickled cabbage, and when she leaned over the tub she looked from behind like a great bay mare having a drink. There was no nonsense about Rosie. If the chapel wanted a scrub, if anybody required laying out, or if a chimney had to be swept, then Rosie was called in. She would survive the strike if it went on for five years. When the dust settled Rosie would still be ponching. With such a diversity of skills, and a back as strong as a crane, she was as indispensable as the pit-head winding gear which she somehow resembled.

Sam Watson peered into his quart pot. "We don't want no bloody bullock-roasting this time, neither." He glared at Bill Swain, the landlord. "You let them roast that bullock at the back of this pub. Ought to have burned your bloody place down."

"You were quick enough to gobble it down you, you can eat ten taters more than a pig," Bill flung back at him.

Tony Pandy was listening hard. He was a refugee from some scandal or other in South Wales and his real name was lost in his past somewhere. He lived on his own in the "Forty Bridges" a great viaduct which ran through the valley. The arched supports were hollow and several people lived a troglodite existence inside the brickwork. He was as Bolshevist as Trotsky and preached his gospel of 'Share with your neighbour' at every opportunity. He was quite willing to share the comforts of his dark hole with anybody. If they could stand the smell.

"What's this bullock-roasting, Samuel?" Tony was given to using everyone's correct name in full.

Sam Watson paused. He had a most aggravating habit of slowing down the conversation when he had someone's attention. "Why, in nineteen twenty-one it were." Pause to sink half his ale. "John Waverley, the crafty sod." Pause whilst he looked round the room to make sure that everyone was listening. "Got Norman Booker, the Manager, to roast this bullock at the back here." He paused again, while his eyes rolled upwards in piggy ecstasy. "I can taste it now." He smacked his lips so noisily that Tater Varley could stand it no longer and broke in quickly, "Ye like a bloody great fool, Sammy. Shut your gob and I'll tell him. Everybody were short of a meal and Booker announced this bullock to be roasted. Everybody turned up to watch. Not ta eat, mind, just ta watch. Well, this 'ere bullock, it smelt that grand. First one and then another 'ad a taste and then we were all 'ard at it and that's 'ow they got us back."

"Well, you didn't have to go back, just because you'd eaten his meat," Tony Pandy shouted up.

There was a deathly silence whilst Tony looked from one to another. What had he said? "You didn't have to go back," he repeated.

"Oh yes they did." Bill Swain spoke up for them. "Like taking the King's shilling."

"We swallowed 'is bloody bait", said Tater and slammed his pot down. "Another quarten, Bill. Let's sup some bloody ale before this strike starts."

So the conversation left the imminent strike while the business of living went on. They would be told what to do when the time came. They paid sixpence a week for cleverer men than themselves to look after their interests. They knew that the whole of the T.U.C. was behind them. It was a comfortable feeling.

And so it was that on Tuesday, May the fourth, nineteen

twenty six the T.U.C. called its members to support the miners and the battle was joined. The men had brought up their tools and stowed them in the coal-houses. The pit ponies were brought up the shaft with bags over their heads until they were clear of the cage. They were still blind for a considerable time, even when the bags were taken off, the unaccustomed light being too much for their eyes, and they walked into hedges and trees in a state of bewilderment until at last they began to see. The sweet young grass was a pleasant change from 'chop'. They lived on chopped hay and oats whilst down the pit. The hay was responsible for introducing rats and mice. Whole generations of rodents were born and died in utter blackness. An alien world, without food or light. Fitted only for *homo sapiens*.

TWO

Jobey sat on the platform looking at Joe Bird's restless brown boots. They were dusty and creased, rather like Joe's face, which resembled a well done crusty loaf. Joe Bird no longer had the suet dumpling pallor of the miners. He had addressed so many meetings he had a face like Father Christmas.

"Not a penny off the pay, not a second on the day", was the rallying call. His passionate voice swelled over Jobey's head to reach every last man of the thousands of miners who had walked to Hucknall to hear him speak. This was a General Strike, not just the miners, so from to-day there were no newspapers, no buses, no services that were not essential to life and security. The workers were solidly behind these men in mufflers who stooped forward now, collier-fashion to hear their champion speak.

"We will start with a prayer, brethren. Show everybody we're not bloody heathens." The shuffling and the spitting came to a stop, while Joe Bird put up his arms towards the heavens and reminded the Lord of his promise that the meek should inherit the earth; he then carried straight on to matters of a more immediate nature.

"You may well ask, brothers, what the Federation has done for you, apart from calling for a strike and taking your sixpence a week. Well, for a start it got you a cage to get you up and down the shaft."

There was a chuckle from here and there.

"You laugh, brothers? Well, when you've had a good laugh, remember this – less than a hundred years ago your grandfathers were going up and down on the end of a rope and not so much as a canopy above them to protect them from falling stones. Men were fished out of the sump and put into a bag to be buried ... what was left of them. And if they got down to the seam safely, they could be working in a heading no more than three feet high. Children pulled tubs and skips all day long in that hell because there wasn't enough height for a pony. As you stand here to-day, brothers, in God's clean air, I want you to remember that. I want your hearts to bleed for those men and kids, because mine does. I want you to harden your hearts and know who you're fighting, because we're a bloody long way from home." Joe began to lay it on – he was often carried away by his own rhetoric, but he was determined that this time he would stoke up their boilers. He went on.

"Some Owners don't see fit to employ a man unless he signs a document denouncing Union activity. I know a place where, if you cause any trouble, the first thing you know you've been put on the market. You all know what it means to be a market man ... you can only work if some other poor devil is injured. That's good for discipline, the butties 'll tell you. Well, that sort of thing's got to stop; we're going to be treated like men from now on. Men who won the War for Mr. Waverley and his fine friends. Nearly half the miners in this country went to War in '14...'18, that's not bad for a reserved occupation, eh?"

He paused for a quick breath, "The Owners and the Government have declared war on you ... the working men of Britain. We don't want any bloody hymns about the Lord keeping us in our proper station. We have as much right to a joint of meat on Sunday as anybody. There are men in this country who would see the collier's standard of life degraded so that Owners' wives can attend fancy dress balls so loaded with jewellery that a flunky has to follow them around with a chair."

Joe had been reading his local history and had certainly fired his own boilers. This was gutsy stuff, and one or two of them could have knocked up a guillotine then and there. There was not a sound to be heard as the crowd hung on to his every word.

"Listen men. Listen hard now." He paused with a finger in the air. It was a warm day which heralded a long hot summer. Not a bird chirped, not a dog barked. "This is how it is throughout the length and breadth of the land. Your brothers are with you in Durham, in South Wales, in Yorkshire, and not only that – for the first time, the whole of the country is with you."

There was a spontaneous thunder of applause which went on for over half a minute. "We have them this time, men. The whole country is behind you. We'll show 'em. We'll get the minimum wage. Control our own ballots and to hell with their talk about non-Union pits. Shall I tell you a story about non-Union pits?" He shuffled himself back into his coat – he had almost climbed out of it in an excess of enthusiasm. "About once upon a time when there were no safety officers? When Owners declared that if any Mine Inspector went down the shaft they would wall him up?"

Jobey looked humbly at the solid boots which were somehow attached to the voice spell-binding this great mass of hard men. He shuddered at the thought of all those faces turned his way, and squirmed a little closer to Joe's legs.

"Boys starting work at six years old minding doors. There was this strap arrangement which fitted on the head for pulling tubs when they were a bit older. They were thrashed by the butties and God knows what hours they worked.

Barrels of beer placed for men at the pithead, which washed the coal dust down and also steered them straight to the nearest pub, where the Company had a vested interest of some sort. Men paid in vouchers to spend at the Company shops, where everything was thirty per cent higher than anywhere else. Union meetings held in secret where the fireplace had to be addressed as "Mr. Chairman" to avoid leaders being identified.

We were so quaint and novel that two miners were paid to appear on the stage in London, just as if they were walking home after a shift, pit dirt and all. Well, they'll happen not think us so bloody quaint now. What few buses and trains were still running have been stoned to a standstill and folks know we mean business this time. We might have been a bloody joke once to these extra specially civilised people in the Government, but to-day we've got the whip hand."

"That's before yo wa' born mester. Com up ta date with thee."

The voice broke in during a slight pause. Hundreds of heads turned toward the owner of the voice. A bull of a man in a black flat hat, with a neck as thick as a horse. He could well have been planted by an Owner to stir up trouble.

He had picked a wrong moment. The miners were a long way from giving in yet. Hadn't they got the T.U.C. behind them? For the first glorious time their brother working men were helping them out. It was a wonderful feeling to be living in such enlightened times. Thanks be to God that ordinary men from Jarrow to Westminster were holding hands and forming a protective wall around the underprivileged colliers.

Joe pointed a finger at him, "How would you like your little children to work down the pit?"

" 'Aven't got none," the black hat returned.

"Then bloody shut up for somebody that has." The crowd went mad, cheering and laughing as if the strike were already won and the Owners suitably chastened. Joe Bird had them in the palm of his hand. If he had fed them all with five barley loaves and two small fishes there wouldn't have been a raised eyebrow.

Black-hat heaved his large square body towards the platform. He had a walking stick of sorts which looked more like a shillelagh. From the expression which emanated from his broken nose area, he meant business. Joe stamped his foot twice, and Jobey got to his feet. Planting himself between the two men he raised a fist like a smoked ham and twisted the stick from the owner. Snapping it like a twig he offered the man back his two pieces. There was a roar from those close enough to see, as the man turned tail and strode off without a word. Jobey sat down again at once, his face as red as a beetroot at being the centre of attraction. Joe Bird put his hand down and squeezed Jobey behind the neck, who hunched his shoulders into a huge, shy smile.

Tater Varley had seen it all. He and his mate Charlie Wildgoose, a man who really loved his pick, had walked seven miles to hear the great man speak and they felt rather proud that Jobey was one of themselves. They were having a good day and had yet to eat the two chickens they had pinched along the way and sat and plucked in the cemetery.

The meeting broke up in good spirits and the pubs in Hucknall were very soon dry as the Band-of-Hope Meeting House. Good humour was the order of the day. They had all had their batteries charged by the oratory of Joe Bird, and the weather was good.

Joe, however, was feeling anything but good. He took himself off to the side of the canal to watch the youngsters swimming. He threw a stone at the bloated body of a dead dog which was caught up in the reeds, and the more he thought, the more troubled he became, knowing only too well the weakness of organised labour.

He knew there was no money in the kitty. The nineteen twenty-one trouble had only just been paid for. Five long years to straighten off the Federation debts it had taken, and now they were starting the biggest confrontation of their lives with hardly a penny to their names. The Derbyshire miners were going to lend them ten thousand pounds but this would only act as an anchor, holding them fast in the middle of stormy waters when the going got rough. Joe Bird was a Midlands' man and he thought 'Midlands'. The coal was easier to get there. The Midlands would suffer a lot less than most, if each district was left to negotiate its own agreements. Joe was also a realist, he knew it was the practice of most Owners to employ more men than they really needed, to be able to meet the peak demands of winter. In the summer a bit of a lay-off suited most Owners very well, and summer was coming on.

There was no shortage of able-bodied men and no shortage of British coal. The Government appeared to be more than ready to take on the colliers, and this made Joe Bird uneasy. If the miners were prized away from the protective safety of the T.U.C. then the fat was really in the fire. He recalled 'Black Friday' only too well; the miners and the railwaymen and the transport workers had made a triple alliance for a mutual support, but when the crunch came on that black Friday in nineteen twenty-one, the miners had had to go it alone.

He watched a patch of scrubby hawthorns giving slightly into the wind, adapting themselves to this stony barren area. They were looking quite well in spite of it all. How many of the colliers at Hucknall to-day would blow with the wind? The country had given them the whip hand – at the moment – and they were going to whip the Owners – it was 'the dawn of a new age, a bloodless revolution'. The miners were counting their chickens.

His thoughts came back to the present. The pits were in a deplorably rundown state, productivity per man going down instead of up. The Government were determined to stop issuing a 'Dole to the Inefficient'. Elected leaders were picking up the big stick to show who was running the country. There were grandiose statements from hot headed young men without families to keep, 'They can beat us to our knees Brothers, but we'll never give in.'

Brothers ... Brothers. How that word did ennoble a lost cause. Did a Captain call his ship 'Brother' as he went down gloriously with it? Did Hunger Marchers feed it to their empty bellies as they marched on Westminster? Would they shout it to each other for the next generation as a very poor substitute for proper Union protection? Because Union credibility would sink lower than a pit sump if they didn't pull it off this time.

Joe could have wept for them all ... but mostly for himself. He was already branded a malcontent by the Owners, but if they lost this fight he would be castigated by the Federation, also.

He addressed himself, with the hawthorns for audience, "Joseph, lad, you're on a bloody good hiding to nothing, here."

* * *

Young Freddy Honey, eyes active for mischief, greeted his bosom pal Dick Prentice. He and Dick had a killing to attend.

Butcher Barnsdall paid them sixpence each to help kill a beast every Wednesday night. They also got half a bucket of blood each, which they took home after the killing. It had to be constantly stirred with a wooden stick to prevent it going jellied. In hot weather the flies were a nuisance but the precious stuff was at last got home and into the copper. Black puddings were never the same from a shop.

They could smell the blood now as they approached the slaughterhouse. Everyone knew this was what drove the cows mad, and that's why Freddy and Dick had to help pull with 'Barney' on the rope.

The Butcher was waiting for them.

"Get the rope round its neck, Fred, and watch your arse-end for its horns." Freddy slipped the noose over the horns, which looked very hard and solid. Barney was in charge and held the pick in one hand while they laid the rope out and passed it through a big hole in the slaughterhouse wall. They now had to haul the beast into the slaughterhouse and pull its head through the hole as if it were looking out to see what the commotion was all about. The noises it made were awful to hear. It seemed to know it was taking its last few breaths.

"Pull, lads, nearly got her." Barney strained at the rope as the bold terrified eyes stared hard at them. A last all-out heave, and the head was through. Freddy whipped the rope a couple of turns round a stake, while Barney raised the pick. Hesitating a second to get the range, he drove it hard at the cow's forehead. This was the moment the boys had been waiting for. With a mixture of horror and primitive satisfaction they heard the bone go. They watched the knees buckle and the open eyes go out of focus, looking, but not seeing. No noise now, the terror in the beast's trembling frame was past noise. Only Barney moved. Pulling hard, he withdrew the pick from its forehead and inserted a cane. Freddy never asked why, but Dick said it was to rattle the cow's brains about and finish it off quickly.

The job was done now, but Freddy heard the forehead caving in many times in the quiet of the night. He looked into the great glassy eyes which stared from the dark corner where the cracked mirror stood. He teased the nobler, more sensitive part of his mind by dangling the horror-stricken image of the slavering cow's face in front of it, until he had a strange compulsion to see and hear it again.

In his fifteen short years, Freddy was one of life's losers. Life dealt so harshly with him that he was given to persecuting himself during the dark hours of the night, so that what happened during the day would not seem quite so bad by comparison.

He felt into his straw-filled mattress as he lay with his mind dwelling on the rigidity which a mortally wounded animal seemed to adopt. His fingers closed over the flea he was seeking. He brought it up into the light of the candle, expertly flicking it into the hot wax. It spun around twice, they always did that, and then it was still. Was it dead? Killed by the shock of the molten wax. He hoped not, he wanted it to suffer.

Fleas were not nice, he hoped it was still alive, imprisoned with its family from the night before, who were all still there, obscene specks on the smooth white belly of the candle. His hand went down to his thin buttock where he could feel another contender for the wax.

His bony fingers traversed the weals across the small of his back where the six strokes of the birch were still engraved as clearly as they had looked twelve months ago when he received them at Lincoln Prison. Freddy made many an apple core for himself by dropping his trousers to display the marks, like the staves of a chair back. Not that he was proud of them, it was just that his stomach was never full.

He looked at the claw-like appendage he had for a left hand, it was a strange arrangement of bones and entirely useless except as a sort of hook. Flora, his mother, had stared horror-stricken as Mrs. Green held up the newly-born baby and pointed to the deformity. Freddy had hardened through now. Could hold his own with any gang on the street and had come to terms with his hand.

His mind continued to jump about. There was no work tomorrow. He promised himself a hunt for rats in Butcher Barnsdall's yard.

Barney paid a penny for every rat which Freddy caught on the premises. Freddy cut off their tails as evidence. A few months earlier he had tried to retrieve the previous week's tails, in the hope of being paid again for the same work. He had been rumbled and got a thrashing for his pains. He decided against any more 'get rich quick' methods.

* * *

Over the next ten days the common gardens had never seen so much activity, the miners being the most gullible people on earth for gardening lore. They enjoyed the mystique of nature and there were fairies at the bottom of every garden, living cheek by jowl with the eternal pig being fattened up for Christmas or Hill Top Wakes.

Seeds were dressed with snuff to keep the pests away. Soot was dug in to keep the devil away from the parsley. Pea-sticks were stuck in where there were no peas, just to fool the birds.

Things had to be set on the wax of the moon, or was it the wane? It didn't matter, so long as you made a fuss about it. If you were going to grow something bigger, and grow it faster, than the next man, then you had to show some enthusiasm.

The pigs thought their time had come, and, indeed, as the days went by, for some of them it had. 'Checky' Bailey was sticking throats by the score, five shillings a time. Those who wanted them killed at home just put a rope round the pig's nose and walked him off. 'Killer' Calladine decided to have Percy salted down. He often sat and talked to the pig for hours, and sometimes walked seven miles to Nottingham for a sack of cheap crusts. He did not have much in the way of food scraps and scrounged for Percy from everyone in the neighbourhood. It was customary to repay the neighbours at killing time, but if Killer had done the right thing he would have had nothing left but the squeal. But Killer wouldn't recognise the right thing if he fell over it.

He walked Percy along the street, heading for home and the killing bench, tears rolling down his nose as he listened to the familiar grunt.

"He trusts me," he sobbed to Pop Rainbow who was just off to the "Dog and Fox". "For hours I've talked to Percy and now he's for the knife."

Pop clapped him on the shoulder. "Bring him in for a last drink then, Killer. Got to see him off properly."

So they took him into the bar, where Percy blew so hard down his snout, the sawdust flew about like a sandstorm. They put him a pint down but he knocked it over. Bill Swain, the Landlord, was not very keen on a pig in his bar, but Killer and Pop were good customers.

Killer was not to be consoled. The more he drank the more desolate he became. "Brought him up from a runtling, that little jockey," he moaned.

Pop aimed at the spittoon. "Taint nothing but a pig."

"Nothing but a pig? He's just about the best friend I ever had, that's all." Killer leaned down and put his arm round the pig's shoulder. "There's something fine about this pig." His voice was slightly thick as he continued to drown his sorrows. "Pigs is nearest to humans, you know." He swallowed hard. "Pigs is nearer to humans than some people I know." He nodded wisely, looking into the air to avoid giving too much emphasis to the remark by staring at anybody in particular. "Got to see him off proper. A man don't have that many friends that he can afford to eat one. Look at his lovely pink skin, fair glows, that skin does." He slapped the pig and a cloud of dust rose into the air.

"Who let that pig in here?" An uncouth voice grated across the room from the bar. It was Freddy's father, Bert Honey, on his way home after two weeks living rough in Mansfield. He had saved just enough for a bit of dutch courage before going home. "Sithee, the gormless bugger's brought a pig in, Bill," he complained to the landlord. "He wants bloody locking up."

Killer took up his stance in front of the pig. "If I give this pig the word, he'll clear this bloody bar in two minutes."

"What, him and another pig?" Bert Honey roared with laughter. "There's him and another pig, they can fight any two pigs in Moorgreen." Bert Honey tittered until beer and saliva ran down his chin. He pointed at Percy who was still clouding the sawdust about. "Clear the bar with his stink, that's about all. I wouldna' eat a slice of bacon off him if I was starving."

"Ya not having none. Ya not having a hair off his back." Killer bobbed up and down in his rage. "Come on, Percy, into God's clean air." He pulled the pig through the door and Pop Rainbow followed him into the bright sunshine.

Percy was in the mood for walkies and set off at a brisk trot in the right direction. Killer went all maudlin again.

"Look at the little darling. Never done nobody a bad turn and trusts me to look after him. Me, the very one that's leading his throat to the knife. Got no feelings at all, that Bert Honey. He had hold of Martha at the back of the "Dog and Fox" a couple of weeks back. Well, you know she only charges five bob, and here's Bert Honey slips two pennies in her hand knowing she'd think they were half-crowns. She never knew till she got home and lit the lamp."

Pop Rainbow shook his head. "He'll go and spoil it for everybody. Besides it's enough to make a woman feel cheap." Pop tut-tutted, "It's his wife I feel sorry for. He goes on the rampage for weeks at a time and then comes back with a yard of tripe as a peace-offering. She ought to ..."

Percy pulled up rather sharply. Too sharply for Killer who had a built-in time lag between his brain and his legs. He went sprawling into the dust outside Robey's, the Newsagents' shop. Killer and the pig looked into each other's eyes for a long second until a placard caught the old man's attention.

"T.U.C. says Back to Work!!!" It screamed at them. Back to work – so the General Strike was over. After only nine days the ultimate weapon of the T.U.C. had been withdrawn. The elected Government was back in the driving seat, which it had never really left. It had been inevitable, a government had to govern or what had they fought a war for.

The suffering had been self-propagating and had now blown itself out with a chill wind which sent a ripple through the miners' ranks. They had a fleeting glimpse of possible disaster, of retribution and victimisation of the bold spirits who had spoken the loudest. They listened more closely to the lay preachers. Being mainly Primitive Methodists they were on the extreme left wing of the hosts of the Lord. They had been brought up to believe that the Church of England was just the Conservative Party at prayer, and the miners wanted no part of it.

Oliver Purdy, better known as the Beggarlee Bulldog, was their favourite 'Ranter'. A collier himself, he believed that the Lord helped those who helped themselves. Hell-fire and brimstone filled most of his sermons. He had an unholy alliance with Matty Wilson, bone-setter extraordinary, and they ran a sort of private clinic amongst the willow trees at Beggarlee Brook. Faith healing, bone manipulation, brain washing and mustard plasters. They threw the book at all and sundry who attended the clinic and woe betide the sufferer who did not get immediate relief; they were dipped into Beggarlee Brook rather sharply until the scales fell from their eyes and the germs were washed away by the blood of the Lamb. The ice cold temperature of the water also contributed to the curative properties, and the Bulldog's reputation for faith healing continued to spread. There was no charge for these instant miracles but a flat cap was left in a conspicuous place at every session.

THREE

It was at this time that Jobey Rainbow's life took its all important turn. Out of the blue came a letter from Mr. Booker, asking him to call at his house the following afternoon. It was just a few lines, but Jobey read them so many times he knew every mark on the paper. What could the Manager want with him? Did he know about Margaret and himself? Was the Doctor planning some hair-raising escapade in the deserted mine? He scarcely slept all that night as his mind twisted and turned.

Margaret was bound to be there. Should he pretend he didn't know her? He couldn't do that. His love was a visible, tangible, pulsating emotion. Even now as he strode up the lane towards the house his legs felt as if he was up to his waist in water. The sun was warm to his broad straight back and seemed to light up the lane as a thousand points of light danced from new green leaves all about him, but Jobey saw nothing except Mr. Booker's house. To be near Margaret drove everything else from his mind. Girls seemed so flexible, able to mould into a man's frame and snuggle in with a pulse-quickening movement which lingered with a man and interfered with his normal thoughts. Jobey suddenly made up his mind that women were quite marvellous.

Mr. Booker was in his greenhouse, for which Jobey was at once thankful. He didn't fancy blundering about in the house, which must contain expensive things like vases with flowers, and books, and Lord knows what other obstacles to be knocked over. He pushed his way through a rhododendron patch, treading on some polyanthus and violas which were much too inconspicuous for a man of his size. He loomed up the wrong side of the greenhouse like a rogue elephant, peering inside at Norman Booker, who nearly dropped a magnificent geranium he was staking.

Booker was once again impressed by the immense size and strength of this man. He must succeed with him this afternoon, there was no-one else half as suitable.

"Come in Jobey, come in man," he shook the hand which felt like the business end of a shovel, and planted him down on a box. He was much too big to have in a greenhouse really, but better here than in the house. If he got through the door at all he would be bound to sweep everything down the passage before him. Norman Booker had spent most of the last week in the house and Mildred was already giving him a hard time. He got straight to the point; they had no common ground other than the business in hand.

"Jobey, I have a proposition to put to you and I don't want you to make a decision too hastily." Jobey crossed his legs, felt the box giving way and uncrossed them again. That was a fine fuchsia on the bench behind Mr. Booker's head. The flowers had small party dresses, starched to perfection and the colour laid on as thick as a bull's ear. His eyes roamed around with only a flicker in the Manager's direction.

"Jobey, you are listening, aren't you?"

Jobey nodded quickly. "Yes, Mr. Booker."

"I'm offering you work, Jobey. I want a security man to protect the pit and its buildings. I want you on our side, Jobey, and I'm willing to pay. There's a cottage goes with the job, and you'll be on the staff. I'll give you time-and-a-half your present pay and you'll have a secure job for life. Enough money for you to get married, Jobey. Get yourself a girl and live happily ever after."

For the first time Jobey looked at Booker. What kind of a suggestion was that? Booker was smiling at him. A big, warm open smile. No, he didn't know anything. There was no suspicion in his mind, or that friendly smile would not be there.

Jobey thought about the proposition. "You mean now Mr. Booker? Right now while our strike's still on?"

"Course I do, man. It's now we're likely to get trouble, eh, Jobey? You do know the other Unions have all gone back to work, don't you? The colliers are on their own, but the Owners have the Government on their side."

Jobey frowned, and tried to think further. "Why doesn't

anybody want to help us, Mr. Booker? We've never hurt anybody. Why doesn't the Government like us?"

"It's a long story, Jobey. Don't bother your head about it. Just say 'Them', not 'Us'. You'll have to learn that in this life, Jobey, there's always an "Us" and a "Them" and it pays to know which side your bread's buttered. I hear you're the muscle man for Joe Bird. How much does he pay you, eh? Are you getting time-and-a-half from him? Does he pay the butcher? A chap like you can't live on home-rendered lard. Does he slip your old man a drink? There's a long, hard struggle ahead, Jobey, and when it's all over we'll have lost our sales overseas, half the pits will collapse into the gobbings and nobody between here and Durham will have a brass farthing. Food vouchers issued which'll keep all colliers poor for twenty years trying to pay back. Do you think the Owners would ruin themselves if they could afford the Federation's terms?" He was on his feet now, quite carried away by the force of his own arguments. "Think for yourself, Jobey. Don't let anybody lead you by the nose. I'm asking you to help us see those colliers have a job to go back to when this is all over."

Jobey swallowed hard and looked at the Manager, his face was like a St. Bernard in pain. "Mr. Bird said the Owners could afford it. He said we should stick together and we would win."

"Never seen a balance sheet in his life, the bloody fool. Anybody would think the Germans were paying him to stir up trouble. He's got ..." The Manager stopped short as Jobey raised a finger the size of a banana.

"Joe wouldn't take no German money. No, I've got to stay with the men, Mr. Booker." The remark about Joe Bird had been a tactical mistake. Booker felt like kicking himself.

"Come again tomorrow, Jobey. Think if over, and not a word to a soul, eh?"

"Won't be no good, Mr. Booker. I'll take the job after the strike, not before then." Jobey was on his feet now, ready to go. The Manager plucked a pelargonium flower and put it in Jobey's button-hole. "We pass this way but once, lad. Get yourself some of the good things for a change. You'll be a long time dead."

Jobey's eyes roamed round the greenhouse, admiring the

clouds of colour which hovered above the shelves. The fuchsias were his favourites. He saw them every year at Moorgreen Show, roped off from the crowd, exotic and a million miles away. Now they were near enough to be touched, and they called to him like a siren on a rock.

His interest was not lost on Norman Booker who picked up a small plant of 'Mission Bells', deliberately making the pendulous flowers swing a little.

"You want this, Jobey?"

Jobey pulled the plant to him. He had always wanted a fuchsia. The delicate flowers of such perfect symmetry excited some deep emotion within him. Some chemistry inside him responded to its thrusting flamboyant beauty. It was all he could never be ...

"Come back tomorrow, Jobey, and take your pick."

Jobey opened his mouth, but Booker pushed him outside. "Tomorrow, Jobey, come back tomorrow."

Jobey got to the bottom of the lane and sat on a stile to hold his buzzing head. He didn't notice a slight movement behind him until a hand came over his eyes.

"Guess who!" The hand was as smooth and scenty as the bar of new soap he had once been given for Christmas. Whose but Margaret's? Now her hands slid down and her arms were tight around his chest. "Now I've got you, Jobey Rainbow. I'm going to carry you off into this wood and squeeze you to death."

His heart leaping with delight, Jobey jumped off the stile with Margaret clinging to his back with the lightness of a cloak. He swung her round his neck as if she were a lucky charm on a chain. He put both arms around her and pressed her to him in silent ecstasy. Neither of them spoke for a full minute, then Margaret could stand the pressure no longer. "Give me air, let me out."

Jobey's smile lit his whole face. He chuckled to himself deep inside his chest, saturating his senses with her nearness.

"What did you say, Jobey? Time-and-a-half, a Company cottage, a regular wage fifty-two weeks every year." She took hold of his scarlet ears and shook his head with them. "What did you say to that then, my man Jobey?"

A small bomb seemed to explode in his stomach. He relaxed

his hold as if she had suddenly died in his arms. He heard a small voice from inside himself saying "I didn't take it, Margaret. I couldn't. I couldn't."

She looked at him. "What did you say, Jobey? Have you taken the job?" Her words echoed back off the empty air as Jobey hung his head in silent misery. He let her go and she turned away from him, twisting her hands in a bitter silence.

The breeze outlined her figure against the flimsy dress. Every exquisite line showed soft and rounded. The gentle swing of rich chestnut hair caressed the line of her neck, arched as it was, whilst she watched the new grass, washing its waves up to her feet. Jobey stretched out his hand and touched her shoulder. He was lost. If they lynched him for it, he could not deny his love and lose this one chance of happiness.

"Margaret, I'll take the job," he said flatly. He was never very articulate and now he felt overwhelmingly sad and quiet. She turned to him and they pressed close together, neither of them speaking; rather as if there had been a bitter argument which they had both lost.

"I want you to take it because *you* wanted to, Jobey. If you take it just to please me it will always come between us. You'll hate me when the men start to hate you; when they call you scab and blackleg; when the women beat pans and tins as you go by; when every friend you ever had hopes the roof is going to fall in on you. Your life will be empty, Jobey, and you will blame me, because I emptied it for you. I'll feel so guilty I'll want you to hate me. If anything happens to you, I'll hate myself. There's only me to take the place of all this, only me to fill the gap. What shall we do when the honeymoon's over? Oh, I don't know what's to become of us. Hold me close, Jobey, ever so close, so no-one can hurt us."

He held her firmly, spreading his fingers out to embrace her in their comforting strength.

His ponderous brain kept turning over what she had said. The gap without her in his life would be much greater than any temporary breach between them. If the whole world turned against him, he must have Margaret. He took the flower out of his button-hole. "For you," he whispered. "It will only die, with me. You will keep it alive, like our love."

She knew that, for him, this was eloquence indeed. The quickening wind raced into green turbulence all around them. They stood alone in the fresh spring air, in a new world, born only a few weeks ago; it was a fitting cradle for a new-born love. It was a Garden of Eden, but as they both knew, it was a fool's paradise.

They could see down into Moorgreen, to a forest of pit-heads which were unnaturally still, to the grimy terraced houses where men were starting an impassioned battle to hang on to their toe-hold of decent living standards. Down there, the only thing life had to offer was their collective strength, cemented with their loyalty, their love of fellow-men, their hatred of the turncoat. Their motto was "Bear ye one another's burdens," so boldly embroidered on the banners they carried at the miners' annual fete.

Jobey knew all this by instinct. He belonged there on Engine Lane where he had been born, where they built up an immunity against love and tenderness and similar nonsense, where the coal carried its message on the wind and laid down a thick layer of dust which seeped into all hopes and dreams like a soporific blanket.

"God help me!" breathed Jobey. His crime was loving too much. His sentence was yet to be passed.

FOUR

Jobey dressed slowly. He pulled on his pit trousers, heavily lined with black lisle stockings by courtesy of Corrie, Matty Wilson's wife, next door. The knees were patched inside, several pairs thick. How should a Security Man dress? He gave it up and settled for his ordinary pit clothes. Bread and dripping sandwiches in one pocket of his coat, bottle of water in the other, muffler tucked into his shirt, and hands deep in pockets, he turned away across Engine Lane, heading for the pit.

There was a hedge of sorts which divided the small front gardens from the road. Stunted and sparse it filtered out its daily ration of pollution from the heaving atmosphere around the sidings which had been stacked solid with coal. John Waverley had stock-piled for the last six months, and was in no hurry to sell. There was a good time coming for those who had a bit of coal put to one side.

The hedge survived, according to Oliver Purdy, the Beggarlee Bulldog, only because the good Lord had placed the stomata holes, through which the plant breathed, on the underside of the leaves. In His infinite wisdom He had seen this situation arising since before time began. Had He not created the very forests Himself for turning into coal? It was not likely, then, that He would forget to make provision for such conditions.

The fact that these forests must have been older than the Garden of Eden itself was not for good Primitive Methodists to question. The Bulldog was a bundle of energy in the service of his Master, one could not have everything. Sunday tea-time was a peak in his religious fervour. He liked nothing better than to invite a gathering of friends to tea, and then berate them, over the home-made scones, in his holy temple of a house where no divorced woman had ever set foot.

After tea there were hymns around the piano, recitations and Bible readings by the Bulldog. It was only right that he should do all the talking. After all, it was his cucumber-and-onion they had been putting away. The cucumber-and-onion were sugared, salted, covered in vinegar and put into a big glass dish which he had won at Hill Top Wakes. It was the bulldog's favourite meal, and if he was on his own he opened a small tin of salmon which sat on top of everything with succulent majesty. When he had friends in to tea they had to use their imagination with regard to the salmon.

By the time the Bulldog had finished reading they had all had their morale stiffened harder than their collars. If anyone had ever dropped a pack of cards on the table, the roof would have fallen in on him instantly.

Jobey had been to one of these teas a fortnight before. Being warm, and pleasantly full, he had been dozing quietly on the well-scrubbed form at the table when the Bulldog went into action. Springing to his feet, he knocked the table flying.

"Do you believe in the Lord, my sons?" he thundered across the room.

"Yes, yes," came various surprised answers to his question.

"Then stand up, and fight for Him," the Bulldog roared. His arms were high in the air, pulling up his braces to reveal his wrinkled brown boots. A trace of spittle ran down his chin and the glare in his eye was enough to stop a charging rhinoceros. He was on a collision course with all the sin in the neighbourhood.

The others all stood up, looking around self-consciously in case they had missed someone who was wanting a fight. After about a minute the Bulldog unfroze and they carried on with what was left of the tea. What did the Lord say about blacklegs? Was the Bulldog for him or against him? Was it scones or scorn?

The hedge thinned out as Jobey approached the railway crossings. It looked as good as any other hedge this morning. It had stood holding its breath all night whilst the frost fitted each twig with a bespoke coating of silver. It was like Christmas day. No-one about because no-one had to work.

"You going to work, Jobey?" The cold, brittle silence shattered in a cloud of silver frost as Mrs. Frogson swung open her gate on her way to the "New White Bull" where she cleaned the brass work and emptied the spittoons. The question was followed by a scream of incredulous laughter at the sheer unlikelihood of her own question.

"That I am, Mrs. Frogson. Starting today, on Security." The words fell flat at his feet. Mrs. Frogson rejected them. Her foot actually poised in mid-air, showing a twisted stocking and turned-up pointed shoe. Jobey continued on to the pit, walking away from Engine Lane and the place he called home, marooning himself on a small, black island, whilst the tide rushed in behind him. Could the treasure he sought be recompense enough for a way of life he had lost?

Almost with his ABC he had learnt the meaning of 'blackleg'. If a man was seen coming from the direction of the pit and was suspected of putting in a quiet day's work the colliers grabbed him and pulled up his trouser legs. In these days before pithead baths the man may have washed his hands and face but his legs would still be black. If they were, he received short sharp justice for strike-breaking. He was quite literally a blackleg.

Mrs. Frogson's disbelieving eyes followed him to the silent menacing pit head, bitterly abandoned by two thousand impassioned men; to an atmosphere so charged with emotion and hate that she wouldn't have thrown a stone at it herself. She sucked in a breath and shook her head, unconsciously using a phrase she had heard the miners use many times, "There be Dragons, Jobey Rainbow – There be Dragons".

Mrs. Frogson was to be relied upon to spread the word. It would lose nothing in the telling.

* * *

Tater Varley was in the chair. Charlie Wildgoose and Sam Watson were waiting for instructions, and the Beggarlee Bulldog was licking his chops.

"It's my land I tell you. I hold my clinic here and if you chaps want to dig for coal, you'll have to pay." The Bulldog leaned on one of his willow trees, prepared to haggle all morning if necessary. Sam Watson played a tune with his fingers on the handle of his spade as he waited for the horse-dealing to finish. They were going to dig for coal on this bit of land which belonged to Oliver Purdy, and Tater had declared himself Chairman of the Board. Sam spat on his hands in readiness, knowing that if the Bulldog haggled much longer Tater would hit him with the spade. It was quicker than taking a vote, and, in any case, it was no use being Chairman if you couldn't get your own way.

"You get a quarter share, same as us," said Tater.

"What about getting it in writing, then?" The Bulldog was not for trusting anybody.

They ignored him and took off their jackets. They would pay up when the time came; they all knew that, the miner was a man who never broke his word.

Charlie Wildgoose summed it up. "There's a time for praying and there's a time for digging. Now leave us be, parson." He stuck in his spade and threw the clod of earth in the general direction of Lantern House, where the Waverley Brothers lived in splendid isolation. "Stick that up your jacksy, Mester Waverley, we've got a mine of our own now."

Charlie was small, square and generally silent. He saved his every grunt to smash at coal. He had a built-in compulsion to ripe into any large lump of coal, and nothing in life gave him the satisfaction he derived from striking hard at the coal face. It had just the right sort of resistance. The splintering sound which deepened into a bony "ZOK" was good to a man's ears. The expert twist of the wrists which could start a deep split and expose the grain of the coal, looking almost like the deep flesh of a wound; the new coal smell was not just imaginary. He had never married. His emotions were all centred around the coal. He often worked through 'snap-time' if his pick was working well. On the days he did stop for snap he rested the pick haft on his loins and drummed on it with his fingers. The solid straight graining gave off a sound from inside itself which found an echo in Charlie's lonely heart. He was an artist, whose only canvas was a record for hewing coal that only the great Tater Varley could equal. But now the pair of them had brought their picks up, and were looking round for something on which to spend their strength and zeal. This outcropping wasn't the real thing, but it was coal, of a sort.

On the other side of the brook another party had begun to

dig. Pokey Jordan and Sid Perkins were also after the coal. The sweat ran down Pokey's great hairy belly as he stopped now and again to swing his cunning piggy eyes at Tater and his party. Pokey could sink enough beer to float a canoe without once relieving his bladder. When he finally did go, he stood back about three feet from the wall, hands behind his back, staring at the ceiling. He grunted and sighed as his distended organs got relief. As Sid Perkins used to say "He sounds like a bloody great station hoss ..."

Sid Perkins had met him in jail. Pokey was doing a stretch for robbery with violence and needed a look-out man while he worked over a few friends who were a little hesitant at handing over their tobacco. When it came to the in-fighting Pokey was as mean as a pole-cat. He was quicker than a striking snake when it came to gouging an eye or biting off an ear. He had a knee action so swift and accomplished that many a man had lost his appetite for sex for years after Pokey had finished with him.

"How deep *they* got, Pokey?", Sid Perkins gasped as he flung out the clay.

"Shut up. Keep digging", Pokey replied. Sid lodged with Pokey and his family. So long as his board was there every week Sid was in. But ... Sid kept digging, he did not want to lose *any* of the comforts he received from Mrs. Jordan.

Nobody expected to reach coal the first day, but they made about eight feet straight down, and at last Tater called "Time" for the day. Without a word they took themselves off to the "Dog and Fox" where they each had their own quart pot. Made of local clay and salt-glazed, the pots were as personal to a man as his false teeth. The first quart "Never touched the sides" so they set them up again.

"Come and take the top off this, Pop", Tater invited Pop Rainbow to drink from his pot, a mark of affection reserved for the best of friends. Pop took the top and plenty of the middle, grunted, and returned to his seat in the corner. Bill Swain filled the pot up again whilst Tater was staring very hard at nothing, in the opposite direction. If a man perpetrated a little act of kindness he had to cover it up by a rough tongue or an abrupt action. It was part of the rules. Otherwise he displayed a chink in the armour of tough exterior they all affected.

Martha stood outside the Pub waiting for it to get a little darker. She did not have enough money for more than one drink, and could not ply her trade in the daylight. If she had enough money to get in the Pub for one drink she could take it from there as a rule.

Pokey sauntered up with Sid Perkins and sized up the situation. Never a one to pass up the chance of a bit of a laugh, he picked up Martha so as to reveal her patched and faded bloomers.

"Have a look at next week's washing, Sidney," he roared, then dipped her back-side in the horse-trough. "First bloody wash it's had in a month," He exploded with laughter again.

Martha dare not strike back. She knew Pokey's reputation. Man, woman or child, he knew bestial tricks for causing them pain, which decent people had never heard of. She bit her lip and stored it away. She might catch him drunk one day and knew just what to do if she did.

Pokey entered the bar still laughing and clearing his throat with a practised noise. He emptied his mouth visibly into the spittoon in front of Tater, slapping a shilling on the bar and glaring at the landlord.

"They tell me they've started going back at your bloody pit, Varley". His voice carried to all corners of the room, as he intended.

Tater eyed him with obvious disgust. Pokey worked at Low Park Colliery, about a mile from Moorgreen.

"What are you talking about, Pokey? There's no scabs at Moorgreen."

"Pokey drained his quart pot and belched. "Not the way I heard it. You've had one man turn up for work today that I know on. Only wants one rotten apple."

"Who's workin'? If somebody's at work, I've a right to know. If not, then shut your gob."

Pokey thrust out his face towards the other three. "I'll tell you who's workin'. I'll tell you." He paused then, not taking his eyes off Tater. He was inviting someone to ask him again. It was a Moorgreen man was letting the side down, and he was going to rub their noses in it. No-one spoke, so he asked the question himself. "Who's workin'?" I'll tell you who's bloody workin'. Your precious Jobey Rainbow. That's who's workin'."

The "Dog and Fox" took a half-minute off while everyone repeated the statement to himself several times. Charlie Wildgoose had his mouth wide open, then recovered. "I don't believe it. What's Jobey doin' at work? Who says he's at work, anyway?"

"He's your new Security Man and been at the bleedin' pit all day, in case anybody wants trouble. No bleedin' kids to keep, no house round his neck, but it's times like this a man shows his true colours. His colour is yellow. He's surrendered in quick time. He's bloody given in before the strike's bleedin' started. How many'll be at work tomorrer, eh? The rot's started at Moorgreen." The leer on his face was so strong his features appeared to be dripping on to his chest.

"You lying bastard. Get back to prison, where you belong, you poisonous scum". Now, prison was a subject that was never, but never, mentioned to Pokey. All eyes spun round to the speaker. It was Pop Rainbow, his frail body trembling with rage.

Pokey walked over to Pop's corner, his red eyes taking in the bundle of wreckage that had once been a man.

"You smell, old man. You smell with a smell that sticks in my craw." He threw his half pint of beer that was still in his pot straight into Pop Rainbow's face. "I'm going to wash your mouth out in that bleedin' horse-trough that I've just dipped Martha's arse in, and it's plenty good enough for you." He extended a muscular arm with whipcord veins and grabbed the old man's throat. The next second he was flat on the floor, having given his cheek bone a smashing blow on the corner of the table as he went down. Tater Varley stood behind him with a stool in his hand. He had hit Pokey with it behind the knees. It was surprising how it fetched a man down. Pokey pulled himself up. "You've asked for this, Varley. I'm going to take you apart so slowly I'll make you beg. You sod! I'm going to make you beg in the middle of this room." His voice was so compressed by his rage so that he hissed like a snake. He did not hurry. His hatred was cold and clinical and loathsome. No flush of anger or flurry of action. He was a true sadist who could hand out a thrashing for the pure joy of inflicting pain.

He threw off his clothes as he stood his ground, watching

Tater. He was built like a tank above the hips. He had not been down the pit for several weeks but his body was covered in coal muck which had worn into his skin, and in parts been eroded by sweat. His body resembled a piebald horse in colour and shape. He was consumed by a trembling venomous streak, and it showed as he circled slowly towards Tater.

Tater stood four square and rock still. His slightly bowed legs, which had never run from anything in his life, were bent at the knee to give him speed of movement. He knew that if Pokey got the better of him he was crippled for life. No-one interfered. No-one breathed except in short shallow gasps in case it should break the mens' concentration.

Pokey's hand came in contact with a quart pot. He flung it into Tater's face, at the same time kicking viciously at the knee cap. The quart pot was badly aimed so Tater let it go, concentrating on lifting his studded boot to take Pokey on the shin as the foot came at him. As the studs ripped down to expose the shining white tibia bone Pokey's face puckered up with the awful shock. He shook the leg several times and the blood made patterns in the sawdust.

Pokey came in again, grappling for any sort of hold, and the two bodies came together like a collision of railway engines. Quick as lightning Pokey got a leg behind his man, and they sprawled on the floor with Pokey on top, smiling grimly. He struck a cruel blow with the edge of his hand, aiming straight at his opponent's throat. It was a killer blow and Pokey knew it. He was so incensed, he put in a death blow without a thought for the consequences.

Tater beat it by a fraction. He pulled down his chin and took it on the bottom lip. It split in a burst of blood and the loosened teeth showed through the mess. They lay together for a few seconds, Pokey trying to thump Tater's head on the floor by gripping his hair and snatching it back.

At this moment the door burst open with a bang that almost pulled it off its hinges. Before anybody could move, Pokey had been hoisted into the air like a side of bacon, hustled through the door, and flung bodily into the horse-trough. It was made of stone and weighed about three hundredweight, but Jobey cocked it over, trapping the unfortunate Pokey beneath it. He managed to wriggle away at the cost of a large area of skin, and didn't go back in for his clothes. Pop Rainbow had been home to check on Pokey's story, and his head was still wet with Pokey's beer as the story unfolded.

Jobey took himself back home as Martha watched from the shadows. As Pokey got to his feet she put the hat-pin away. There was always another day to deal with enemies. Jobey knew this too, and knew also the seething hatred which Pokey harboured, which would fester inside him. Moorgreen was not big enough for the two of them, now.

A few minutes later he heard Tater next door at Matty Wilson's, having his lip stitched back into place. On a sudden impulse he walked into Matty's operating theatre. It was normally a kitchen, but when Matty put on his striped apron it was transformed. There was no ceremony of knocking on doors. Nobody had anything to hide, and sex was strictly for cold dark bedrooms.

Matty had a yard of gut on the needle and was pulling it through with a great flourish. The Beggarlee Bulldog was in attendance as usual. They worked together whether neutering dogs, extracting teeth or concerned with darker work. Rumour had it they could solve problems for young ladies who had been indiscreet; but that Mrs. Frogson would say anything.

The Bulldog had a grip on Tater's head like they had when the sawed the horns off a cow. Jobey looked into the pain-filled eyes.

"Just came in to say thank you."

"Didn't do it for you", Tater gritted through his mangled lips. "He did it for Pop," added Matty. "You want something? Everything's 'secure' here."

He had been welcome at Matty's house ever since he had been born, and the words came like a slap in the face. His brain was numb and he felt his self-respect running down and leaking out through his boots. Fighting he understood, but insults from friends hit him from the inside. He had not the wit to marshal his thoughts into arguments. He was out of his depth and he knew it. His eyes came to rest on Oliver Purdy, Beggarlee Bulldog, Man of God, Leader of the Primitive Methodists. Jobey looked at the Bulldog with the puzzled, hurt look of a child. Beseeching a word from this neighbour;

from this friend; from God. From anywhere in earth or heaven, but all he got was a blank stare. A condemning silence built up in the room, ushering him out and slamming the door on his tortured soul. His footsteps crunched on the coal-slack path as he stared into the small scrub of a garden.

A clump of Angelica thrived against the wall of the ash-pit, it could cure anything from fever to bunions, everyone knew that. He could do with a plaster of it right across his heart just now. A straggling honeysuckle showed its promise of things to come. It was pegged into the crumbling wall, which didn't look too bad by moonlight. The garden didn't amount to much more than this, but then neither did any of the others. Every Sunday morning the men walked round, telling each other of the plans they had for the small barren plots. It was just that, well, what with the pigeons and bad backs and broken tools and the next-door cat ... Engine Lane was a hard place to live. He went back inside his own house, to find a bright shilling staring at him from the mantelpiece. One of his thirty pieces of silver had come home to roost.

He set off to find Margaret. The thought of her drove everything else from his mind. She far, far outweighed a dozen Engine Lanes.

She had put the pelargonium flower in a glass specimen vase in her bedroom. It had pride of place, overlooking the garden and the orchard to the dumpy hills towards Newstead. Mildred Booker was delighted, calling husband Norman to come and look at the flower. He paused at the bedroom door, having no need to go nearer, to recognise the soft mauve pelargonium "La France" he had given to Jobey.

"What's the matter now, Norman? She's taking an interest at last. She must have been in the greenhouse and picked it herself. I certainly didn't put it there. The girl's actually been in your greenhouse and thinks enough about the flower to set it up there on its own."

"The flower's got nothing to do with it, dear. It's who it came from that sets it apart."

"What do you mean, Norman, surely it's one of yours?"

"I gave it to Jobey Rainbow when I asked him if he would work during the strike. He's the best insurance I have against damage at the pit-head."

"Norman Booker, if you've cooked up something for my Margaret I'll kill you. I know that great hulk of a man. Lives on Engine Lane with a no-good father. If that's all the ambition you've got for your daughter ... you ... you."

Booker looked as black as thunder. "I'll tell him. I'll warn him off, and you talk to Margaret, but he stays in the pit. He's better than a platoon of the guards, and he's mine, all mine, I pay him. Anyway Mr. Waverley knows all about him now. Thought it was an excellent idea, so there it is."

Margaret heard every word. She had paused under her window to let Jobey get a little nearer the house, half hoping her Mother would see them together. Now it was out of the question.

They met on the slope of Misk Hills again. Furtively, like criminals hatching a plot. Their love made them outcasts from their respective worlds.

They melted together in a hawthorn cave which time and bitter cold winds had carved out of the living bush. The full moon illuminated a wild damson tree which threaded its blossom through their hedge.

"All the comforts of home, Jobey. The wind has even brought us these leaves in for a carpet," Margaret whispered.

"More like for hedgehogs to hibernate." His gruff voice seemed too loud for their tight, secluded hideaway.

"Hush, Jobey, everyone will think you're calling for company. Let's dream a dream, Jobey, about the good things we would like. I want ... I want a house set in fields rolling away in all directions. No neighbours, I don't want any people in my dream. People want to tell you how to live your life. They make rules to stop others being happy. I want to live in a world full of silence – and Jobey Rainbow. Now it's your turn. Both of us have to put something into the dream, or it won't come true."

"I was in a fight to-day, Margaret."

"And then another part of the dream. It's September now, and I look into our house from the lane. See, the fire's painting the room in short red splashes, and outside the leaves are curling into helter-skelter shapes so they have a longer ride to the ground."

"And my Dad put his shilling back on the mantelpiece."

"We've not had the winter yet, Jobey. The snow makes the world like a giant swan's back, and when it's finished snowing and the clouds all lie on the ground, there's nothing between us and the sun. All the better to see you with, dear Jobey, eh?" Her voice changed to a quicker, lower note. "All the better to see the starving and the fighting and the people who point at other people. Don't open your eyes, Jobey. You're not missing a thing out here. Let's be like the coal, go to sleep until times have altered. There's plenty of leaves."

"Well be like hedgedogs" Jobey's deep voice cut in.

"Hedgedogs? Hedgedogs?" She imitated his deep voice. "That's twice you've said that. The word is hedgehogs. Say after me Master Rainbow, Hedgehogs, Hedgehogs." She ruffed his face in her hands and spoke the words closely to his lips.

Jobey's face was scarlet with shame. It was a word he had always mispronounced when he was young.

"Anyway, hedgehogs find it very difficult to make love, we don't." She rolled under him and suddenly the embarrassing moments of his youth seemed very small beer.

And so the enchanted moments went on, under a moon which knew its business. They would both remember this night on Misk Hills for the rest of their lives. Just as Margaret intended they should.

* * *

Jobey was reliving every moment of that moonlight tryst the following day, when he had a visitor at the pit. Freddy knew what it was to be alone and unloved, so he turned up to give Jobey some support. "My Dad says nobody's got to talk to you, Jobey. Says Joe Bird's coming in with some men to get you. How many men can you fight at once, Jobey? I told them there wasn't enough miners in the whole country to beat you, Jobey. But they said they could throw stones and you couldn't dodge them all. I've come to cheer you up a bit before they get here."

Jobey chuckled aloud. "There, you've made me laugh already, young Fred." He tossed the lad a slice of bread and dripping. "I'm pleased to see you, Freddy, but you mustn't come again."

"Why not, Jobey? You're not doing any work. If the men come for you I can run for help."

"I've got a telephone for that, Fred." Jobey pointed to the wires, not knowing they had quietly been cut half an hour ago where they entered the trees of Watnall Wood. He looked towards the trees as a movement caught his eye, but he dismissed it as a deer.

"Can I telephone for you, Jobey? Can I turn the little handle?" It was about time to make his routine call from the lamp cabin so Jobey nodded his head and Freddy picked up the instrument between finger and thumb as if it might electrocute him. "What shall I say? There's nobody answering. It's not talking, Jobey. Why won't it work for me?"

"Because it knows you're on strike, Fred."

Freddy looked at Jobey, who managed not to smile. "Give it here, lad." He cranked the handle and listened, looking through the window at the trees. Again he saw movement. Quite definitely now he knew someone was watching from the trees. He looked at the dead instrument in his hand. "They're coming to get you, Jobey" was what Freddy had said. He put the instrument back on its cradle and went outside. Leaning against the brickwork of the top of the shaft was the trunk of a sizeable pine tree which he had chopped for this purpose. He spat on his hands and picked it up. "Now, Freddy, you get off up the side of these trucks and keep going. Nobody's going to throw at you."

"But I want to help you, Jobey. I can ..."

"Get off now, or you'll be the first to feel this." He whistled the great piece of trunk above his head, and Freddy took to his heels up the sidings.

Pokey Jordan happened to be on those very same sidings which sloped down sharply to the pit-head where Jobey kept watch. Quietly he lifted up the heavy brake-arm on one of the full trucks of coal and let it free to hurtle down the slope to the pit-head – and Jobey. He had left his partner, Sid Perkins, in the trees to give warning of anyone approaching. There was no-one else anywhere near the pit, only Jobey's imagination peopled the wood with irate miners.

The truck gathered speed as it rumbled past Freddy, who

suddenly realised what was going on. He jumped on the wagon, holding the top of the side with his good hand, at the same time putting his feet on the brake-arm and bouncing down with all his weight. He was not heavy enough to get any braking power at all, and the truck hurtled onwards. Jobey could see the truck coming and shouted to Freddy: "Get off! Get off!" His voice trailed away as he saw the speed at which the wagon was travelling, not knowing whether to advise Freddy to jump or to stay. The lad pulled himself up at the side and onto the small coal with which the wagon was filled.

Jobey was helpless. There was a bend in the line at the pit-head, and the truck must leave the rails at this point. In the few seconds left before the crash the only possibility he could see was that Freddy might be able to jump from the truck and into his arms. The thought went, as the truck thundered by, throwing itself outwards on the bend, like a toy. It shuddered along on its side, shovelling its own load before it and picking up another scoop about three feet deep, coming to rest with all wheels off the ground and spinning madly.

Jobey felt pins and needles all over his body but sprinted along to the heap of steel and coal, dreading to see what it had done to Freddy. One leg was sticking out of the coal and Jobey tenderly uncovered him. There was no need for any examination. Apart from probable internal injuries, his neck was broken and the head was in a most unnatural position.

Heavy with grief he laid the body inside the lamp cabin and set off for Sergeant Wheeler and the Police Station. The dispute had claimed its first victim. Conditioned all his life to paying for other people's mistakes it seemed obscenely natural that Freddy should be the first to go. The eternal scapegoat, born for some reason not apparent and living for a time that was not to be given to him. His death was a mistake, like his whole life, a tiny thread of misery in the tapestry of the coalfields. Even the Beggarlee Bulldog, who could manufacture a reason for most of the Lord's work, was at a complete loss for once, in a silence that was more telling than anything he could have said.

The question of the telephone wires being cut was serious. Sergeant Wheeler could not connect the two matters but he could not ignore the coincidence. Could the truck have sprung its own brake, or was it realeased?

Norman Booker had no such doubts. "It was deliberate, Jobey. Whoever did it was hoping to damage the pit-head or discredit you." He laughed bitterly. "I won't ask if you have any enemies, Mr. Waverley has a few men coming from South Wales who will be helping you in a day or two. He wants to speak to you himself, after Freddy's funeral."

It was not the sort of day for laying a young boy six feet under the ground. The sun continued to shine as if determined that Freddy should have something right before the world was done with him. The Waverley Brothers were both in church, in what had once been a private pew and, in fact, still had its own fireplace.

Most of the miners who knew Freddy attended the service. Many of them wore their war medals as was customary on any ceremonial occasion. Sergeant Wheeler was in great evidence, convinced that if the truck had been released deliberately the man would be there, and somehow give himself away. He was right about the first part. Pokey was there, and as the miners filed past the grave he looked up into Jobey's eyes. Jobey had stationed himself at the head of the grave and watched the procession file past. As Pokey brought his eyes up from the coffin his conscience troubled him for the first time in his life. As the two men looked at each other Jobey suddenly knew. He knew as certainly as if he had seen the man release the brake.

The knowledge was stored away to ferment and add to the bitter feelings which brewed between the two men.

An airship flew overhead as they were drifting away from the cemetery. It seemed like a message from the quick and the rich, that the business of life must go on. It put the funeral into perspective. This was just one life amongst so many and the negative quality of death was its own burial place.

A hand slid past his own and a quick warm squeeze nearly caused Jobey to jump out of his skin. It was so unexpected amongst the brooding, silent mourners. It was Tater Varley's wife, Minnie. Now there was a strange thing. She looked neither to the left nor the right, and Jobey had to reassure himself that he had not imagined it.

She had her own son Steve with her, he was almost thirteen and rather delicate, certainly not a chip off the old block. He held hands with his mother and his eyes were full of tears for Freddy, whom he had known so well.

"It looks a very deep grave, Mother."

"Deep? They're all the same depth son." She held on tightly as he peered into the hole, his skin as pale as marble, his fingers showing up like polished bone. He shuddered and Minnie held on even tighter, throwing around him the thin cloak of protection which exuded from her very nearness to him. Her heart beat heavily as she looked at the coffin and then at her only child. He's nearly a man now, she told herself. Pulling him away roughly they made way for the other mourners. "Kids!" she murmured to a friend, "they bring so much love with them yo' happen to getten fond on it."

John Waverley had his chauffeur stop and pick up Jobey. There was only just enough room for him, doubled up as he was.

"My chauffeur told me who you were Job but I don't think I should have needed telling. This is a bad business, do you think the truck was deliberately released, Job?"

"I don't know, sir – I'm sure I don't know." Jobey couldn't begin to explain to anybody what he knew.

"Did Mr. Booker tell you about some Welshmen I've sent for?"

"Yes sir, he did."

"I wanted to speak to you about that, Job. To tell you why they should come. You know, some of this trouble is in the grass roots of our industry. If only I could make the men see it. They would all be better off if the Unions were non-political. Argue about their jobs, yes, but let the Government get on with the job of running the country. This money from Russia. The poorest white country on earth, why have they sent a million pounds to boost the strike fund? Can't the men see it's a deliberate attempt to undermine law and order? Civil strife is what they are after. If the T.U.C. hadn't called off the General Strike we could have had civil war and a takeover by the Bolshevists. They would have thought that was money well spent. You do see all this, Job, don't you?"

"Yes, Mr. Waverley," Jobey was frowning hard and fixed his eyes on the back of the driver's neck.

"Why do they think their fellow trade unionists refuse to

black the handling of imported coal? Why has there been no levy put on the other Unions to help the miners? These are their own fellow-workers. They know our exports of coal have dried up. A world-wide depression means we shall do well to hang on to what we've got. Gas, oil and electricity are all striding forward. The miner works less hours than anyone else in the country. Your typical miner will earn enough to keep himself for the next week and then he's off with his damned whippets on some business of his own."

Jobey noticed the chauffeur's neck had gone very red.

"Do you know what could happen this year Job? In spite of our shocking bad start? We could make record profits during nineteen twenty-six. Record profits I tell you. Coal is rising to a sensible price at last."

He crashed his fist into his palm. "If we could get coal while the others are still out, eh, Job? That would be worth a bit of something."

He did not say to whom, so Jobey did not know how to take it.

"All this is plain common sense. Why do the men not see it? I must get some men from Wales if only to keep things ticking over. Are you on my side, Job? Do you think I'm right?"

Why was the great man using all this breath on Jobey Rainbow? He felt numb in his head. He didn't know anything about civil war or Bolshevists or export markets. Joe Bird did this sort of thinking for him, and, he suspected, for most of the others. What he did know was that it was one hell of a long way to walk underground, and then get your tools all sharpened and ready, only to be told there was no work to-day. The cry was passed on, "Loose All" which meant there was not a ha-penny to be earned to-day. No attempt was made to tell the men before this stage. The "Market Men" turned up every day of the week hoping some poor devil was ill or had an accident so that they could get a day's work in place of the injured man.

He thought of the men working in a space Mr. Waverley would not send his dog into. All his friends who were old before they were young, getting two days holiday at Christmas and half a day for Moorgreen Show. There was no other holiday because they were not paid for. Men just worked on –

perhaps until they were seventy or more if the roof stayed up. Or until their lungs were topped up with the dust.

He thought of Joe Bird's story of the Owners' wives who went to a ball with so much weight of jewellery that they had to be followed round with a chair. Joe had a favourite saying, "He that hath, shath; He that hathna, shathna." It was a bit of broad Derbyshire, but he could understand broad Derbyshire. He could understand all the immediate things and the impact they made on his daily life, but he buried them deep in his heart for the time being.

He thought of the limousine he was riding in, and of John Waverley who had his private plot in the best part of the cemetery, and meanwhile lived in Lantern House with its three hundred acres of amenity grounds. He longed to tell John Waverley to stick his job up his private fireplace in his private pew. Instead he thought of Margaret, and his heart filled with a love that was greater than his self-respect. She was the one precious jewel in his dark humdrum world. She weighed in the scales more than everyone else in his life.

"I'll show the Welshmen round, Mr. Waverley. What do you want them to do?"

And so Jobey got in a little deeper.

FIVE

Pokey was having trouble with water. He had picked a bad site for his private pit and had stood in water so long now he had practically got webbed feet. He had a varied collection of buckets, baths and containers so that his site looked like the front of an ironmonger's shop. He tried swearing and blaspheming and slinging the clinging ooze at the long-suffering Sid Perkins. Eventually he decided to share out the water with his neighbours, so he turned up that night about ten o'clock, with Sid Perkins in tow. It was a blustery, rainy night and dark enough for the job in hand.

Pokey slithered down the bank of the brook, surprising a big rat which he flattened with his spade. So far so good.

"We dig just here, Sid. Just a channel first of all, then we'll widen it later." Just behind him was the outcropping which had been excavated by Tater Varley, Charlie Wildgoose and Sam Watson.

"We've got to make it look natural."

They dug down to the level of the water, then worked backwards to Tater's pit which was now twenty feet deep and bell-shaped at the bottom where the coal lay. Having made a good trench they laid in it several lengths of drain-piping, ripped only an hour ago from the new Company houses on Waverley Road. This took until midnight. They stopped the trench about a foot short of Tater's outcrop and then filled everything in.

It was soon obvious that the brook was flowing along the underground drainpipes because the water level was rising satisfactorily up the shaft of Tater's pit. Pokey and Sid were covered from head to foot in black slime, so they wallowed in the brook to get the worst of it away, and then set off for home. They sat chuckling to themselves in the kitchen, smelling of cow muck and stagnant sludge as the fire began to steam them dry. Pokey's wife came hobbling down the stairs, "to see what they were cooking", which provided them with the best laugh of the night.

Charlie Wildgoose was the first to arrive at the well which had once been a pit. He stared, mouth open at the now useless hole. The next thing he saw was Sid Perkin's spade. Name carved on the shaft for all to see. The others arrived and stood looking at the spade, which told them all it had seen the night before. It said that the flooding was deliberate. There was no need for any of them to speak. They walked over to Pokey's diggings and made a channel from the brook and flooded him out in broad daylight. It was purely a gesture to let off steam, because it was obvious he had abandoned the work.

"The local dogs'll be pleased anyway," growled Tater. They all laughed, Tater's reference being to Pokey's habit of catching any convenient dog which was around his workings and lowering it on a rope tied around its middle. After two minutes he pulled the dog up again. If it was still alive and had not been gassed Pokey knew it was safe for him to go down. The dog itself, after making its contribution to Pokey's production, was helped off the premises by the toe of his boot, he being a man who had never been encumbered by too sensitive a nature.

It was unfortunate that the flooding triggered off a series of spoiling tactics amongst the outcroppers. The men had been on strike for a long time now, and belts had to be tightened. Coal was scarce and outcroppers were getting about four pounds a ton, which was a great incentive ... for some. Others had bouts of conscience, or were just plain idle. If a man was outcropping he spoke of enterprise, if he was lying on his back he called it strike-breaking.

The temptation for a man to lie on his back was great. The summer blazed on in an unnatural quietness. The men went into the fields to talk to their ponies. The sweet young grass was a new experience for all. There was a guilty feeling in a lot of hearts, so conditioned had some of the miners become to the discipline and routine, they could not take each day and enjoy it as their ponies did. The stillness of their immediate surroundings put them constantly ill at ease. It was Christmas every day. There was a sense of something being terribly wrong. There had to be a bill to pay for all this sleeping and sitting.

Tater felt so uneasy about it all he took a day off and walked into Watnall Woods. He was on the slope of a steep hillside and sat on a log to eat his mashed potato sandwich. For the first time in his life he really looked at Moorgreen. Slag heaps growing even bigger, burning steadily. They hollowed themselves out by internal combustion, leaving a hard crust on the top. Woe betide any man trying to walk on them, he would go through into the slow furnace and be cooked like a baked potato. A sulphurous smoke rose night and day and polluted everything along the line of the prevailing wind. Further afield were the heads of another seven or eight pits. All still, no smoke, no movement. Now that the blackened chimneys were serving no useful function they stood naked in their own filth, defiling the surrounding greenery. They defied explanation now that they belched no smoke, mute monuments to man's devastation through a green and pleasant land. Tater hated the chimneys. The business of a pit should be underground, these were just the exhaust gases of a thousand men.

Away from all the smoke the colours were more intense here, and Tater wished he had been here earlier in the year with Minnie and young Steve chattering gaily with their arms full of bluebells. He remembered the time ... Oh what the hell, he was put on this earth to dig coal. Steve could talk about a dusting of bluebells and how the pollen clung to his shoes, but he'd learn before very long that coal slack clung a damned sight harder. There was plenty of it too, Booker was going to start 'Slack Bobbies' after the strike ... spies who crept about without a lamp, listening, to see if the men were using shovels instead of forks. The tell-tale scrape of a shovel had got many men suspended years ago.

Steve had said the woodland flowers had to finish flowering before the leaves grew on the trees and cut off their light. Tater's light had been cut off for many a long year now, he chuckled, but who needed a light to make seed?

He admired the crusty trunks of the old trees like the rind on a bit of old cheese ... funny how his mind kept turning to food these last few weeks. He pushed his fingers against the bark, God, how soft his fingers were getting, even his 'pick finger' was straighter than it had been for years.

Tater let his eyes wander, taking in a clump of healthy nettles, all starched stiff; full of menace and touch-me-not. He thought of Dobbin who could pull them up with his bare hands ... he made nettle beer and threw in leaves and roots of practically everything he could lay hands on. Dobbin was always happy while he collected his ingredients from amongst the shrubs and long grass. Small wonder really, when you came to think of it, the only other employment he ever got was exploding small concentrations of gas before the colliers started work.

Four o'clock in the morning Dobbin started on that hazardous job, sometimes even before the knocker-up was about. With a great long pole and a small naked light he probed the roof for pockets of gas, creeping forward, soaked to the skin. He kept a barrel of water at the bottom of the shaft in which he totally immersed himself before starting work. A pathetic bundle of wet rags shuffling along the dusty passages like some primitive reptile. Now and again the gas would rip off past him in a searing flash.

Sometimes he unburdened his soul to Tater ...

"You ever been in a car Tater?" he once asked. "I shall get a ride when they put me away. Got enough put aside for that."

Odd times Tater sat with him for a minute or two on the doorstep of the "Dog and Fox", watching courting couples heading for the canal bank. Sometimes Dobbin followed them, even trying to keep Tater by his side by relating lurid details of what he had seen. He craved for affection like a child, he wanted people to see him talking to Tater, he wanted to belong. He had no-one to put his arms around ... he was small and animal and despised.

Tater switched his mind off. He did not want to think about people today, he had brought himself to this strange spot for some other reason. He could not exactly say what it was.

He had never been a man of the soil, knowing nothing of its dumb ways under the trees. He scooped into its spongy texture and could feel the fine peaty stuff in his now softening hand. The earthy, woody smell intrigued him. He poked about with his fingers, here was life in a handful of decomposed leaves, growing more potent all the time on this hillside, that same life force which ensured that the trees survived winters when the cold killer winds tried to bring them down. If conditions got too bad for living the hillside died a little, sending its life-bearing sap deep underground to shelter and husband its strength, waiting for a time which was better than the present.

Suddenly he understood a little of the nature of achievements without the aid of a shovel. Tater decided not to come here again, too little work and too much thinking was no good to a man who worked below ground.

The land fell away to the sandy Moorgreen soil where shire horses plunged their great hairy legs, pulling ploughs, creating patchwork effects. Further along, the ground resembled moon craters. Coal was being fetched out now in quite big quantities, and lorries came regularly from Nottingham to fetch a load and run the gauntlet of lean white men who hid on the steep hills and tipped over as many lorries as they could. The residents of Gilthill were never short of coal. It was a favourite spot for marauding bands who daily grew bolder and yet a little more afraid. Tater walked back in sombre mood, past his own Moorgreen pit which seemed more brooding and menacing than he had ever known it before: 'There be Dragons,' he murmured.

Tater's early years had not been overburdened with too much schooling but he had picked up the phrase 'There be Dragons' from an old map he had retained from those days. Tater used the phrase from time to time. It was so out of character with his solid earthiness that it had somehow become synonymous with him. It denoted unexplored areas – when the earth was flat and men had been glad of a reason for leaving these areas unexplored. It had nothing to do with lack of courage or ambition. It was a statement made with finality. It was unambiguous and stood for no nonsense. It was like Tater – and that was why the phrase had clung to him, though it had passed into general usage round the pit.

* * *

Jobey had about twenty Welshmen to help him, but he didn't see a deal of them. They were billeted in Nottingham and came to work every morning in a lorry. Mr. Booker took them below ground and there they stayed all day. Jobey didn't like to question what they were doing. Mr. Booker had given him some very broad hints lately about staying where he belonged. Perhaps it was just conscience but he fancied that the Manager knew about him and his daughter. Oh, what a damned mess it all was. He looked through the window of the lamp cabin which he used as a look-out post. Someone was heading this way. Surely not – Jobey looked again, his heart turning somersaults and then sinking down into his boots. Yes, there was no doubt about it. Slowly, deliberately, heading straight for the lamp cabin was Joe Bird.

This was the moment Jobey had dreaded all along. The man who, like a father, was his teacher, his friend. The man whose respect he could not live without. Joe Bird had every miner in Nottinghamshire behind him. They followed where he took them. Fearless, far-seeing, incorruptible, yet quietly resolute. No bull-at-a-gate impassioned rhetoric, but a plain straightforward statement of relevant facts. They all respected him for his principles, and to Jobey he was a saint.

He wanted to dig a hole and hide. His great hands gripped the chair back he was holding until the wood creaked. "Joe Bird is coming with some man to get you." Freddy had stood just here and said that. Jobey looked around; no movement in the trees or amongst the trucks. He didn't care how many men he had brought with him, he could deal with them all, if only Joe had not come himself to look into his eyes with that kindly unwavering smile. God, this was awful.

The door opened and Joe Bird was inside, closing the door carefully behind him. Jobey had an almost uncontrollable desire to clasp the man's hand and squeeze his shoulders. He wanted to say, "Forgive me, Joe. Think what you like, but don't put it into words, for if you do I've nowhere to hide." He knew he could not. He had forfeited the love and respect of everyone and knew he must sweat this out on his own. He cringed ready for the onslaught, looked into the eyes which were fixed on him, and then hung his head.

"I've come to congratulate you, Jobey." There was a smile

on Joe's lips. Jobey hung on to the smile with greedy eyes, mouth slightly open, he nodded his head vigorously. "Yes, yes, thank you Joe, thank you." He really didn't know what to say. Congratulate him? What about?

"I hear you've got yourself a young lady at last, Jobey. A fine lass she is, too."

Jobey stared at him. "Yes, yes I have, thank you. Thank you very much, Joe. I've got myself a job, too, haven't I?" He was halfway to giving himself a good hiding. This was terrible. Why didn't Joe get on with it and leather into him? He looked round wildly, as if about to run, and then he sank down on one knee. Joe Bird walked forward and clasped Jobey's head to him.

"Jobey, Jobey, what have they done to you, my son? Bend the knee to no man, Jobey. I wish I had a love like yours to live for. It shines like a beacon in this dark, loveless world. There's a pestilence in this land, Jobey. A plague of hate and greed and all that's worst in all of us. You have something that is given to a very few men, Jobey, a heart so full of love there's not a crevice left for hating. When all this is done, Jobey, it is emotions like yours which will win the day. Thank God there's one ray of sunshine in this whole dark land. But not a word outside these walls, Jobey. This is between you and me, like father and son, eh?"

Jobey felt himself giving way to a sob. "I'm not alone," he whispered incredulously. He took Joe Bird's hand, then stood his great height and smiled his infectious schoolboy smile. "I feel like the Lord has answered a prayer, Joe. Yet I never prayed for anything, wouldn't know how, wouldn't dare after what I've done." He smiled his huge smile again and Joe Bird felt his knuckles fusing together in Jobey's happy hand.

"There's more to life than working and eating, Jobey. Don't you sometimes feel it when you're down there? You're nothing more than a heart-beat in old Mother Earth, and you look up from your grave which you share with the bones of old trees, and you know yourself for a very small piece of this earth. You don't have to look at the stars to feel small – but loving, Jobey, ah, that's something very different. Now enough of this. I'm here in my official capacity. Tell me, Jobey, what are the Taffys up to?"

"Well, that's as big a mystery to me as it is to you, Joe."

"Where are they now?"

"Where they always are, underground."

"You mean they go down there every day and never send up any coal?"

"That's it. Mr. Booker as good as told me to mind my own business."

Joe Bird shook his head. "Down there all day and no coal ever comes up. What about night? How do you know they are not winding at night?"

Jobey looked crafty. "I've thought of that. I've tied bits of string to the cage and the winding house – still there next morning. No, I tell you, there's no coal coming up."

Joe Bird shook his head. "I've got to find out what's happening, Jobey. I've got to get down that shaft."

"Couldn't it just be maintenance work? Mr. Booker says we've got to make sure there's a pit for you chaps to come back to."

"Not likely, Jobey. You've seen these chaps. Scum of the earth. They're not maintenance men, they're strike-breakers. Couldn't get any sort of a job in normal times. Enforcement men, employed to turn some poor devil out of his tied cottage, anything that decent men wouldn't tackle, seen the inside of half a dozen prisons. They're pissed as a load of newts every night down Nottingham, knee deep in chips, ale and fanny, running riot with a pocket full of money. They're not getting that for twiddling their thumbs six hundred feet below ground. Your ordinary Welsh collier wouldn't touch them with a knocking-up pole."

Jobey stared at his feet. "Well I can work the cage, but I daren't leave the top. I have to ring the police station every hour."

Joe looked thoughtful, "What if Booker sees the wheels turning and comes to see what's happening?"

"I can tell him some story. One of the Taffys comes up sometimes."

Joe looked at the big honest face in front of him. "You'd be a damned poor liar, Jobey. Let's hope he doesn't notice anything."

They walked to the winding house, Jobey unconsciously on

tip-toe. He pulled up the steel mesh door to let Joe in, and then threw the switches. The cage never made such a noise before. It rattled and screamed to the whole countryside that it was carrying Joe Bird down the shaft. Of all people! John Waverley's arch enemy. Whose side was he on, anyway? Well, it was done now. He'd planted a cuckoo in the nest now, right enough. He brought the cage back and went out into the sunshine. Joe was on his own now.

* * *

There was absolute silence at the pit bottom. The thick dust deadened Joe Bird's footsteps as he set out for the coal face. He stopped to adjust his lamp and heard a sharp rattle from the direction of the stables. With a puzzled frown he fumbled his way towards them, his keen ears cocked for the slightest sound, ready to shield his lamp or turn it out altogether. There again was the same noise. He caught his breath sharply, the strong ammonia smell of horse dung. They had ponies down here! There were three in their stalls and fresh horse manure in several more. He whistled softly to himself and carried on. He must be extra careful now, he would be given short shrift if he was found. If a man was put in the gobbing he was lost forever, he wouldn't be the first man to disappear without trace. No-one knew he was here except Jobey, and he couldn't very well admit that he knew. He began to sweat a little.

This was a fine pickle to be in. He had never thought he could feel so out of place down a pit. It all seemed so unnatural. For the first time he became aware of his termite existence and all the merciless weight above him. This was foreign to him. Had he been away from the pit too long? Would he have to be led down with a bag over his head?

He moved forward again with the practised stoop of a seasoned collier. Eventually he heard the familiar sounds of a coal face being worked. The full tubs were heading away from the pit bottom into the old workings at Westwood. This part of the pit had not been used for years and was served by a long upward drift instead of a shaft. Of course! Fool that he was. Why hadn't he suspected this before? Coal was going out up the gradient to Westwood. The exit was not much more than a clearing in a private wood owned by Thomas Waverley, the Chairman's brother. The sidings had never been taken up and full trucks from here could be infiltrated into the main sidings at Moorgreen. He had no need to look any further, he knew all he needed to know.

Joe looked round for a means of escape. Two full trucks were ready for pulling away. If he could climb on to one of these and throw out some of the coal he would be carried up the drift and shunted among the other trucks outside. No-one about just now so he wriggled in amongst the coal, to await the gangers.

He lay for an hour until he thought he could stand it no longer. A great lump of coal was thrown up onto the truck and landed straight across his face. He could feel blood running down his cheek and into his mouth. He knew the wound would heal with the coal dust still under his skin. The blue scars were trademarks and nothing to be ashamed of.

They were moving now. Thank God he would soon be out of this. The slope was steep but not very long, coal was near the surface here. He wondered if these lines had been left in for this very purpose. No, surely not. He must not allow himself to become bitter and read an ulterior motive into everything the Owners did. That was no way for a responsible Union man to think.

He longed to look over the side of the truck. He could tell from the sound that there were two horses pulling, but were they on their own? No-one had spoken, but of course if a man was leading the horses he would have no-one to talk to anyway. A local ganger always talked to his horse, but these men were foreigners. He began to make up his mind that the ponies were on their own. He shifted his leg, which surely must be broken in several places by now. In doing so, he started a miniature landslide and coal cascaded off the truck. The ponies stopped. Now for it. If there was a man with them he was bound to look at the truck which had shed its coal.

Nothing happened. The slope was steep and the ponies could not hold this load for long. It was like being checked halfway up a switchback. What the devil was going on? He had to rear up and have a look. Cautiously he poked his head over the side, and nearly swallowed his adam's apple. About three inches from him and staring straight back, was the most surprised looking Welshman Joe had ever seen. He was urinating on the side of the truck but grunted to a full stop, blinking his eyelids ten to the dozen.

"How do you do," said Joe.

The Welshman opened his mouth, looked away quickly, and then back at Joe Bird as if to convince himself that there really was a face in his truck.

"Who are you?" he managed at last.

"Here's my card," said Joe. With that he brought a sizeable piece of bat down on the other's head and settled all further argument. "I get more like Tater Varley every day," he muttered to himself, climbing out of the truck.

He wedged a scotch under the wheels of the truck and then released the ponies. Walking back, he kicked the wedges of bat from under the wheels and the trucks went careering down the slope. A message from the Union Secretary to the blacklegging colliers at the bottom of the slope.

As the thunderous crash came echoing up the slope he turned to continue on foot. He could see the exit at the top, and framed in a small patch of daylight were several men who had obviously been attracted by the noise. "Damn and blast," he whispered, but continued up the slope. There should be a man-refuge hole before long which he could press into and hide. He was banking on the dark background they were looking into, making it impossible for them to see him.

There were no refuge holes and the party of men were now upon him. Joe kept going until they saw him. Even then he still kept going.

"Down there," he gasped, pointing downwards. "Get down there and give a hand. Roof's gone". They looked very curiously at him but continued on down the slope. He knew that as soon as they discovered their injured comrade they would be after him.

Joe was not very big but he was all muscle. He was out of the top before they started after him, then he put his head back, tucked in his elbows and went like a well-oiled machine. One of his most treasured possessions was a cup on his sideboard for winning the miners' road race three years in succession. At the age of fifty-five he was way past his best but the short-legged Welshmen were no match for him. He gained the safety of the village and started to organise a meeting for that very night.

* * *

There was a piece of common ground in the village which was known as the Donkey piece, several acres of land which had never before seen so much activity. Most of the outcroppers had concentrated here, and one man, Philip Burgin, had shown the true entrepreneur spirit by making his mini-mine big enough to employ fifty men. The biggest item of capital expenditure was on wood for shoring up the sides and the tunnels. Each night foraging parties went out and lifted whole lengths of fencing from where it was serving no useful purpose, such as dividing the properties of the well-to-do, or keeping cattle off the main road, or containing pigs in a field. The boards were dropped down the twenty foot shaft and immediately put to use before the ubiquitous Sergeant Wheeler raised any objections. Burgin's tunnels extended so far from the bottom of the shaft that there had been several encounters with black damp, and the men were often pulled out unconscious. He wrote to Doctor Alexander at the colliery who was now confining himself to laboratory experiments, since Norman Booker had told him not to risk Jobey again until the strike was over.

Surprisingly, the Doctor turned up to give his advice. His mission was to save lives and a small thing like a strike was not allowed to interfere. He was horrified by what he saw. There was no ventilation of any sort, and he advised an immediate cessation of all work down Philip Burgin's mine. But the men were driven on by the thought of unpaid bills, by children who needed shoes and by throats which were cursed with a raging thirst. The coal was right there before their eyes and beckoned them on like cheese in a trap.

Ted Button was in the trap when it sprang. Rosie had spoken to Philip Burgin herself and got him the job. She knew Ted had a weak chest, but this coal was only twenty feet below ground, and the five kids all wanting new clothes for the

Chapel Anniversary. Ted was in there alone when the silent gas got him by the throat. His weak chest quickly succumbed and he folded over without a struggle. It was so terrifyingly easy.

They pulled him out and winched him up on the mangle rollers which they had fixed for hauling out the coal. They used baths, buckets, bags; anything which held coal to wind up and down the shaft. Colliers were not very good at do-it-yourself. After a day's work down the pit a man got his dinner down him and stretched out on the sofa if he was lucky. If not, it was on the hearth with a rug pegged from old clothes for a bed. The only clean bit of skin showing was a "Nigger Minstrel" area round the mouth which had been washed down with the rice pudding.

Ted Button had done with rice pudding now. Even Philip Burgin was sickened at the sight of Ted hanging from the mangle with the rope round his waist, looking for all the world like a young beast newly slaughtered.

For the first time in her life, Rosie faltered. The five boys she had taken in her stride, from cobbling their shoes to warming their beds with the oven shelf. They fetched her to the Donkey piece where Ted lay on an old door. He looked peaceful, as someone in the crowd remarked. She was conscious of their solicitude for her but they could only communicate this by a respectful silence. It was not done to demonstrate any emotion, particularly in public. She still wore her flat hat which many women affected whilst working. Ted had been a good husband after his fashion, never a very good provider but the children adored him.

She could see the tiger stripes on his chest and the tears came to her eyes. He did the tiger stripes every day and the boys loved it. The coal from an outcropping is wetter and softer than the hard coal down a pit. It clung to the body like a thick coat of sludge, and Ted used to spread his fingers over his chest and pull backwards to leave a fairly clean impression where his fingers had been. When the black sludge dried his chest was covered in "Tiger Stripes". The boys squealed with mock terror when he threw off his shirt and growled at them. It was a small part of the family routine which belonged inside their poor home. It was not for public gaze. It went with a roaring fire and the toast being browned, with the smell of newly mashed tea and happy well scrubbed faces in the firelight, with the excited nonsensical chatter of children to children.

It was totally wrong on a dead man in public. The final indignity in this public exhibition of death. Well, what was she waiting for? Was she the one who laid them out or not? They carried him back home and put the door on a pair of trestles in the parlour. Rosie knew what had to be done.

That evening she sat on her front doorstep with the cap in her lap. All the boys in bed, and time now to wonder how much the Co-op would charge for putting him away. Charlie Wildgoose walked by and dropped a threepenny piece in the hat. She looked up in surprise, and another dropped in from Sam Watson. In the next half hour it seemed that the whole neighbourhood had some business down Walker Street where Rosie lived. It may have been something to do with Tater's wife, Minnie Varley, standing round the corner, her ample bosom bedecked in a gaily flowered apron. The ample bosom was required, to house a very ample heart.

Ted Button was the second victim of the dispute. Their names would never find their way on to a memorial. They had just died in the messy bitterness of 1926.

Rosie had too much fire in her belly to lie in a cold lonely bed so she filled it full of her own small brood. With an instinct born out of years of clinging together they saw the funeral off with a wall of group therapy around themselves; the only possible way to bury a tiger so beloved of his brood. The children only had one parent now, but there was still enough love to go round.

Into these two or three acres of highly charged emotions, Joe Bird threw his plan. At seven o'clock that evening there were about six hundred men round the small platform he had erected on the Donkey piece. Wasting no words, he plunged straight in.

"I was down Moorgreen today, brothers. Don't ask me how I got there, that's not important. What does matter is that Waverley has opened his back door. The Welshmen are filling trucks as hard as they can go and taking them up the old drift to Westwood. We;ve got a job on our hands tonight, men."

Not waiting to hear any more, Bert Honey detached himself from the back of the crowd and sauntered away towards the pit. He went over the sidings where young Freddy Honey had been smashed up and into the lamp cabin. Jobey watched his coming, and so did Norman Booker.

"Joe Bird's been down the pit today. Says you've got the Taffy's taking coal up the drift at Westwood?" The words were phrased like a question but the Manager ignored it.

"Damn and blast. Joe Bird of all people. Well, he's put his head in a noose if he's admitted that. It must have been him hit Dylan Edwards with a rock. Those trucks he released killed a man this afternoon. Let's hear the little bastard talk himself out of that. Wonder how the hell he managed to get down. Did you see anything of him, Jobey?"

Jobey was staring at the Manager, still telling himself that Joe Bird had killed a man. They could hang him for that. Everyone said the Government was wanting to make an example of somebody. Joe, who was like a father to them all. Joe, who he himself had sent down the mine. He looked at Booker, but the Manager spoke to Bert Honey.

"Yes, yes, what else? Come on Honey, don't let's have to drag it out of you. You're paid for your information."

Jobey looked sharply at Bert Honey. The creep, this carrier of tales from his friends. Paid for his services. He stopped his thoughts in full spate, he, Jobey Rainbow, was also being paid for his services. Bert Honey was buying beer with his money, Jobey Rainbow was saving to buy a woman. God, what a mess all this was.

"They're coming any time now." Bert Honey looked out of the small windows as if expecting the crowd to be on his heels. "Joe Bird said 'We've got a job on our hands tonight', that's all I heard."

"Right!" Booker picked up the telephone. "How many men has Bird got?"

"Nigh on a thousand, I'd say."

The Manager raised his eyebrows. "A thousand? Do you know what you're talking about?"

"I know a big crowd when I see one, Mr. Booker. There's all but a thousand men on that Donkey piece tonight."

Booker whistled and looked at Jobey. "You're going to earn

your money tonight, Jobey Rainbow. If those blokes mean business the police haven't a cat in hell's chance." He got through to Sergeant Wheeler to give him his news.

"I'll get everybody there as soon as I can." The Sergeant's voice was urgent. "I don't know if we'll be in time but I'll let Nottingham know right away. The Inspector's got the Riot Act to read to them. We've been watching the crowd, it's getting bigger all the time. Nottingham may decide to bring the troops in, we've got to delay them if we can. Play for time your end, the Inspector's gone down to the Donkey piece now."

Joe Bird had certainly got his hands full. There had been three fights already in the crowd. Pokey Jordan got himself on to the platform and pushed Joe Bird aside. It was no use Joe stamping his foot this time. Jobey was a million miles away.

"We've got more bloody enemies than John Waverley", Pokey roared. "All this bloody outcropping's got to stop. There's more coal coming off this Donkey piece than used to come up the bloody shaft."

"Get down. Get down you bloody fool," somebody behind him shouted. Another voice spoke up. "You did your bleedin' share before water filled ya in."

"Aye, water and Tater Varley." There was a roar from the crowd.

"Who said that?" Pokey was seething with rage. "If I can find who said that I'll bloody blind him."

At that moment a handful of dirty clay caught him full in the face.

"Smack in his bloody chops. Give him some more, lads."

An anonymous voice egged them on. Mud and clay flew from all directions and Pokey jumped off the stage to get at someone he had seen throwing. Joe Bird was covered in mud but he stood his ground. He held up his hands for silence and after two minutes they had quietened down enough for him to speak.

"Who are we quarrelling with, brothers?"

"There's a lot in what Pokey says," came a more reasonable tone of voice. A general chorus of assent showed that most of those present were in favour of stopping the outcroppers. The same men spoke again. "Why don't the Transport Union black the movement of coal? All these bloody Judases couldn't sell it then."

A lot more "Here, heres" were added to this.

"It's not up to the Transport Union to get us out of this," Joe Bird had their attention now. "We've got to put our own house in order. For every Welshman down Moorgreen there's a hundred Englishmen on top doing the same thing, getting coal." He could see the majority of the crowd were with him and he took a chance. A lot of other districts who had no coal near the surface had been accusing him of letting them down. "Watch Nottingham" they had said at the National Conference. "That's the weak spot, that's where the wall will break." He had sat there taking it all. Not because the men were any less resolute, but because the coalfield was so exposed, the temptation was enormous in this area. Well, he was responsible for these men, he was their leader and now was his time to lead.

"Tell you what, men." He looked at the great sea of faces, there were so many now he could only just make them hear. "Before we settle things at Westwood we'll settle things here." There was the silence now that he had been waiting for. "We'll fill in every last one of these outcrops before we leave here."

A great cheer went up from the crowd as they got hold of pieces of wood or any tool to fill in the holes. Philip Burgin went to the bottom of his shaft and defied them to bury him alive. Charlie Wildgoose threw the first shovelful and all the rest followed quickly. "It's killed one bloody man" shouted Charlie. "Stay there and we'll make it two." Philip Burgin got out with his head looking like a piece of raw meat as all the earth and stones bounced off it. The men were relieving the pent-up emotions and frustrations of three months' duration. They were fed up with kicking a pig's bladder around for a football.

In all that time they had seen their children being fed soup or rice pudding and prunes by various organisations. Their pride as heads of the family and breadwinners had suffered grievously. Every time they lit a cigarette and passed it from hand to hand round the group they felt guilty. They made betting slips and gave them to each other instead of to the bookmakers, to have a bit of interest and see how much they might have won. This last few weeks things had got so bad they stood around the front of the public houses, just to be on hand in case anyone should have the money for a drink.

They were men and they had their dignity. Strong, hard, earthy men, uncouth, a few of them, but men to whom women and children looked for the necessities of life. If the man was degraded the family was degraded. They sank or swam together and the men could feel themselves sinking. It was not funny. Times were hard even when work was to be had, but now ... They were reduced to soaking dry bread in water, drying it in the oven and then dropping it into potato soup. It was a good stomach filler. Children were given a bit of rhubarb or apple to wrap in their handkerchiefs and suck. It lasted longer that way.

And so they filled in the outcrops and when the Inspector of Police, Harry Palmer, got on to the platform to read the Riot Act they cocked up one end of the platform and slid him off into a filthy mud puddle. He got to his feet and folded his paper away. He was enough of a realist to know when he was licked. He stood out of the way while Joe Bird marshalled his forces and walked at their head on the way to Westwood.

And at Westwood stood twenty policemen, truncheons drawn, with Norman Booker and thirty Welsh colliers prepared to fight, and in front of all these was Jobey. Tree trunk and all.

SIX

It was not yet quite dark and Margaret stood holding hands with her mother, looking from the bay window towards Westwood. Margaret was trembling although it was not a cold night. The dark mass of men had moved out of sight now, but everyone in the village knew just what was going on. The women gathered in groups at the end of the entries.

Mildred Booker spoke quietly, she thought now was the time.

"They're both on the same side anyway, dear. The wrong side I fancy, by the look of that ugly crowd, but I'm sure they'll survive somehow."

Margaret looked at her. As an only child she had always been very close to her mother. Her eyes fell on the Bible under the aspidistra bowl which kept them company in the bay window.

"You mean Jobey?"

"Yes dear," her mother replied in her sweet reasonable tone, which was not always a good sign.

"How long have you known?"

"Since he gave you that flower which is in this Bible now."

"Fancy you knowing where I put it. That's not quite nice to be as nosy as that. I don't follow you around the house spying on you."

"You'd have a pretty dull time if you did. If your father gave me a flower now I should want to know what he'd been up to."

There was an awkward silence. They both knew the subject was on the agenda now and must be discussed.

"I'm not going to give him up, mother, so you can save yourself a lot of indirect approach, and oblique references to Ralph Waverley." Margaret fired the first shot.

"I wasn't thinking of Ralph Waverley, though goodness

knows he is the Chairman's son and ever since he finished University he's been making sheep's eyes at you. Margaret dear, have you seriously thought what you will use for conversation? What will Aunt Beatrice make of him? She'll be dreadfully upset, and you know she's going to leave you everything. What *about* money? You'll have none except your own. Don't get serious about him, darling. He's a novelty for you, a passing fancy. I remember when I was your age, good gracious ..."

"Do you know what they're doing now, Mother?"

"You have a most tiresome way of changing the conversation, dear. I was about to give you the benefit ..."

"I think I'll slip on a coat and go to Westwood. Jobey will need me, if there's anything left of him."

"You're making a good start. Hanging around pit-heads to pick up the pieces. You'd better get used to that." Mildred Booker's voice took on a harder tone. "There's a lot of things you'd better get used to. How to blacklead a fireplace until you can see your face in it. You'll burn ten tons of coal a year to dry pit clothes and add your bit to that pall of smoke in the valley. Hot days in summer you'll have that fire going to hot up the oven for dinner, kettle on the hob and saucepans on the fire but the bars on the fireplace will have to shine like ebony. And do you know what's the worst part of all that? Not rubbing your fingers out of shape with the blacklead, or knocking lumps of flesh out of your hands on the fender. No, the worst part of it is that your friends and neighbours will judge you on whether that bloody fireplace shines or whether it doesn't."

Margaret looked sharply at her mother. It was very rarely she had to emphasise a point by swearing.

"Ever since you were tiny we have striven to give you a proper sense of values. Not just a formal education, but pointing out the things that mattered." She picked up Margaret's hand in frank admiration. Sandwiches in her own coarser, spatulate fingers, the hand was like white marble. The smooth fingers tapered to perfectly rounded ends. "Don't you see, my darling, you have so much to lose. You'll never see the sun setting between the sycamores in Watnall Wood, as it does from here. It will just disappear behind the slag heaps, suddenly, dustily, cruelly. And then it will be dark, and people will come in and talk about ponch tubs, and if it is time to empty the pans in the lavatory. And they'll look at your fireplace and then they'll fold their arms and go next door to do the same ..."

She stopped very suddenly, her voice changing back to the softer, well-modulated tone she normally used. "I know. I sound like the original Tory Memsahib, but I just happen to know that the unequal distribution of wealth is a fact of life, and that it's so easy for a mind to atrophy when it becomes isolated from its kind". She looked up and smiled. "There, I've said my piece and never mentioned Ralph Waverley, not once." She broke into a broad Derbyshire accent. "Now if tha wants thi coat, it's in 'all cupboard. But think on."

Margaret smiled, she could do the broad Derbyshire with the best of them. "Aye, Muther, I'll think on." And Margaret went out, prepared to pick up the pieces.

* * *

Jobey could hear the swell of noise in the distance as the great crowd of men drew nearer. He turned and saw Booker who gave him a nod and a smile which was intended to reassure him, but didn't. It was almost dark now. The land they were on was private property, belonging to Thomas Waverley, but nobody kidded themselves about that. This was a violent mob, and anything or anybody standing between them and their objective was asking for all he might get.

A five-barred gate was the first to go. It stood at the entrance to the private road with barbed wire wound over the top rail. The sight of the wire incensed the men at the front of the crowd. It looked cruel and sharp and law-enforcing. The notice above the gate bore the one word 'Private', but today the men saw the small invisible print which was always there, but needed the magnification of three months' lock-out to bring it into focus.

They heard it screaming defiance at them with a deep penetrating voice which had the timbre of local magistrates built into it. The judicial authority of class, and friends in high places. It didn't read 'Private' today, it spoke to each of them personally, and said these rabbits in this wood are not for the likes of you. These rhododendrons that have banked themselves up for years have done so for better eyes than yours. "He that hath, shath, and he that hathna, shathna," so take it out of that.

They did just that. The gate was hand-made with wooden dowels and not a nail in it anywhere, but it broke like any other gate. It broke smaller than any other gate because the pieces made handy weapons. Joe Bird made no attempt to stop them. They left the road and ploughed through a plantation of silver birches. Forcing aside the golden yews, they rushed on through a small forest of pines with their carpet of bracken and ferns. A body could be left here and never be discovered for fifty years.

Suddenly they were on the edge of the clearing where the vital evidence lay in abundance. Full trucks of coal ready for moving to the Moorgreen sidings, coal all on the ground. Good coal, hard, shining black lumps such as no outcropping could yield. There was a quick silence as the appreciative audience took in the sea of coal; connoisseurs to a man, they had not seen its like for a small life-time. They saw the Welshmen, tense, but ready to fight for their pay-packets. The police, who were going to get their heads kicked-in, and they knew it. For the last few weeks the police had been very thick on the ground, and every small group of miners they found they broke up and moved along. Some were unnecessarily rough. As Matty Wilson put it, "They've got a job to do but they needn't bloody well enjoy it." Some old scores were about to be settled.

Cliff Prentice had his eye on a red-haired copper who had done young Dick three times in a year. Dick Prentice, who, with Freddy Honey, had helped slaughter beasts for Butcher Barnsdall, had a sweet tooth and was given to raiding local shops after dark. The last time he had been caught, Cliff gave him the buckle end of his belt. As he explained to the lad afterwards, "I don't mind thi stealing, but tha always gets bloody catched." Young Dick may as well learn right now that the crime didn't lie so much in doing a thing, as in being found out.

Before anyone could move, Norman Booker's authoritive voice filled the clearing.

"Joe Bird. Where's Joe Bird?"

Joe strode forward to meet him, while everyone looked on. Booker kept walking until he stood toe to toe with Joe Bird. "Call them off, Bird. Send everybody home and Mr. Waverley will forget what's happened."

Joe Bird laughed. "Where's Mr. Waverley then? I can't see him with his double barrelled twelve-bore. Isn't it the season for shooting miners? I don't think he's so keen when the game fights back. That's why we've got to talk to the bloody rubbing rag and not to the engine driver."

"Look here, Bird, don't you think you've caused enough trouble for one day?" He lowered his voice. "You're in big trouble, Bird. You've killed a man today with your runaway trucks down the drift at Westwood. That's manslaughter if you're lucky, murder if not."

Joe stared at Booker in disbelief, thoughts crowding through his brain, trying to read in the Manager's face if this was a bluff.

"Call them off, Bird. Call them off, I say, and the Company will cover all expenses. No charges. Just a runaway truck. It happens all the time."

Joe Bird nearly exploded. "You have power over life and death, Booker? The whole of the law of this land comes to naught because Mr. Waverley wants coal? Well, hear this, Booker, I wouldn't call these men off if I could, and what's more I don't believe there's a dead Welshman here at this pit today."

"You've asked for it, Bird, there's not a pit in this country that'll employ you after this, and not only the pits, I'll have every door in every firm within fifty miles slammed in your face. We've done it before and ..."

"Save your breath, Booker, I shall be in jail for twenty years, you said so yourself. That is, if you've got a body to show the police."

"Your name wasn't picked out of the hat for this job, Bird. They picked a man who knows how to hate. Why is it there's always one like you? One who comes from nothing, knows nothing, and poisons the minds of decent men so that they all finish with nothing. I offer to save your neck and you bite at the hand that feeds you, like a weasel.

"Look at yourself Bird, where have you led these men to? You're all at the very brink of catastrophe." He swept his arm towards the now silent, waiting men. "They haven't got a decent pair of boots between them." He stuck out his chin and his eyes blazed. His voice was strained to breaking point. "And they can't win. *You* know they can't win. You've been abandoned, Bird – the Owners have taken you on – and the Government's taken you on. Are you going to wait for suicides? There's some bloody good men in that crowd, and who's rubbing their noses in it eh? It's not me, it's you!" His voice broke with passion. He spoke again, hoarsly. "You can lead them, Bird. You can lead them – nobody else." He turned away, spent and futile, to hear a voice behind him, a voice which had to say the words he was hearing.

"Come on men, we've come to put the bung in the hole. Let's get on with it." Joe unleashed his hounds, and felt like Henry the Fifth at Agincourt. They swept forward, aiming for the trucks to push them down the gradient. The police attacked with foolhardy bravery and were overrun by sinewy men wielding pieces of pitch pine that had once been a gate. Jobey ran to the entrance to the drift and threw some railway sleepers across the line as two trucks came at him, gathering speed all the time. The first truck hit the sleepers and rammed them across the entrance of the steep tunnel, effectively blocking the entrance.

"Just the ticket!" shouted Norman Booker who had stayed by Jobey's side. "What now?"

He had always been the man who gave the instructions, but he had automatically handed over to Jobey. This situation called for a man who understood action and had an instinct for doing the right thing.

"On top of the truck", yelled Jobey.

Booker went up like a startled orang-outang, all legs and arms and his face purple with the effort. Jobey stood astride the coal with his tree trunk, stabbing downwards at anybody who tried to get near enough to push the sleepers away. There was a lull for a few seconds whilst the miners decided what to do. They had a quick conference and then went for more trucks. They were going to try to ram the two trucks down the gradient, taking Jobey and Booker with them.

As the noise and speed of the line of trucks increased, Booker lost his nerve. "Run for it, Jobey, you're not paid to get bloody killed." He jumped off the truck and was roughly manhandled and slung down on top of a pile of bleeding Welshmen. The police, and Welshmen who could still walk, were pulling themselves into the woods to hide in the bracken. Some lay in untidy heaps where they had fallen. It was a very sobering sight to see so many policemen sprawled unconscious in the filthy dust. The miners were normally respecters of the law. Discipline and shortage of money made them creatures of habit, parochial, God-fearing and conforming to a well-tried pattern. Many of them just stood by now, whilst the wilder element raced along behind the wagons, watched by the colossus on his truck.

The wagons came together with a tearing crash, but not with enough force to mount the sleepers and send them down the gradient. Jobey was still there and impregnable. He took the odd swipe at anyone who came near enough, but no-one seriously tried to bring him down.

It was dark now, and in the distance could be seen an army of lorries approaching, headlights full on as they raced towards the scene. As if at a signal the miners quietly merged into the shadow of the trees, leaving the clearing looking like a battlefield, but not having achieved their main aim, which was to block the passage and prevent the exit of any more coal.

There were a hundred and eighty police in commandeered lorries and vans of any sort they could get their hands on, and as they raced into the clearing they made a circle like the old covered wagons, prepared to do battle. But the enemy had fled.

The Chief Superintendant took in the scene, and then he noticed Jobey. "Who in hell's name is that!" he gasped. "Just look at the size of that man. Go and ask him who's side he's on, for God's sake."

But Jobey had seen enough violence for one night. He helped to load up the wounded and made sure there was nothing seriously wrong with Norman Booker, then headed for home.

He had no fears of being waylaid. The miners were all home, and doors bolted behind them. Anyone caught on the streets tonight was in for a real drubbing as the police licked their wounds. Whatever else was said about them, they certainly looked after their own. Massively reinforced, they were billeted on anyone who had a room to spare, and they waged war on the miners for the rest of the strike.

Jobey met Margaret as she kept to the middle of the private road, keeping as far as possible from the bushes on either side. She felt much safer as the convoy of police lorries rushed by, but she felt safer still when Jobey's large frame emerged out of the gloom.

"You're safe, Jobey. Oh Jobey, don't go doing things like that again." His face was black with coal and sweat and the coal dust powdered her face as she felt herself floating up in his arms. He held her so that their faces were level and she pouted her lips and gave him a rubbery kiss. "I don't care if you do smell like a sack of coal. How's Dad?"

"A few bruises, that's all. You shouldn't have come. There's no other women here."

"I was going to carry you home and be there smiling when you recovered."

He felt a bit drained and suddenly realised how tense he had been all night. Now that Margaret had put his world back in order he felt ashamed of the way he had acted. Somehow he sensed that the men had not put their all into the struggle. They had seen the police off, and the blackleg Welshmen, but it had been a bit like civil war after that. Jobey was one of themselves. They had not known how to deal with the situation. The hate had not gone through to the soul. No bricks had been thrown, no dirty tricks, no Joe Bird pouring contempt. He felt a bigger traitor than ever.

Margaret knew the confrontation had shattered him. For all his brute strength he was a happy, gregarious animal, needing friendship and the sense of belonging to the large family. To hate was foreign to him. To be hated was bewildering and humiliating.

"I told you we shouldn't dream about people, Jobey." She stopped and kissed him passionately.

His big smile came back in place. She drew him into her world, giving him back his security.

"Let's walk back through the woods, Jobey. This holy

ground has seen so many pit boots tonight that a bit more disturbing won't hurt."

The pine needles cushioned all sound as they walked through the wood. Suddenly Margaret paused and pulled back on Jobey's hand. "Listen. I can hear somebody in front." Jobey cocked his head but could hear nothing. She stood like a fawn scenting danger. Jobey could have hugged her, then and there. It was only natural, he told himself, that someone so helpless and desirable should have her senses sharpened as a defence mechanism.

They went forward on tip-toe for a few yards until they were able to make out two forms bent over in a small clearing. Jobey steadied himself on a pine branch which immediately snapped off and gave them away. The two figures sped off into the dark wood, leaving a shovel behind them.

Jobey kept Margaret close under his arm and went to investigate. The men had been digging a hole in the soft peat.

"What are they up to?" He asked the question more of himself than of Margaret. "Trying to hide something here. Something quite big."

They looked down at the hole and quite suddenly Margaret gave a quick shiver. "Jobey, don't you see what they are doing?" She clung a little closer to him and looked around at the surrounding dark trees. "Jobey, can't you see?" He looked at her frightened face and then back to the hole. "What is it, Margaret?" His voice dropped to the whisper she had used.

"The shape, the shape." She seemed afraid to put her thoughts into words. Jobey still looked down with a puzzled frown. "It's a grave," she whispered into his ear.

He looked again, nodded slowly. "It might be. It's about the right shape." He looked all about him, concerned that Margaret should be with him. "Come on, let's get you home first. I'll take this." He plucked the shovel from its heap of soil, then stopped. "If it's a grave, where is the body?" Margaret shuddered. "Oh Jobey, let's go. I'm afraid. Even with you here I'm afraid. Even with you here I'm scared out of my wits. What am I, Margaret Booker, doing here? Jobey Rainbow, you can take me home, right this minute, or I'll push you in that grave with the other body. Now what made me say that? Why don't I keep my ...?"

"Margaret, you've got it. You said the body was already in the grave. They're not digging it out, they're filling it in. It's in there, right down here at our feet."

"Jobey," Margaret started walking away. "Take me home, please, I feel sick. My head hurts, and I'm scared. Please, Jobey, I want to go home."

He ran to her side. "Of course, of course. I'll take you home, right now." Putting an arm round her he almost carried her away. There was something enormously protecting about having an arm like that round her and she felt better already. Jobey caught sight of a movement to his left, but said nothing.

It was the slim young figure of Steve Varley, trembling visibly and wondering if Jobey had recognised him. Why on earth had he not told his father that he had been earning a bob or two in Mr. Booker's garden? Why on earth had old Jim, the gardener, chosen Steve Varley to help dig a grave? If Jobey had seen him, he was for the high jump now, his father would not take kindly to this.

He went home quickly, his heart heavier than at any time in his thirteen short years. He was in trouble which even his mother couldn't save him from this time, all for trying to curry favour with Mr. Booker, all for trying to keep himself from having to go down that great frightening black hole.

Any day now Mr. Booker would say to his father, "Bring young Steve next Monday' ... that's the way it was done. That's all that would be said and he would be doomed. He had been hoping for a chance to present himself when he could ask for a job in the office, or in the garden, or anywhere else on earth except that terrifying pit where the darkness would settle on him like the black cap on a judge. That's why he had been helping Jim, in the garden, recently. There was always the chance of being taken on as an apprentice.

He went in to take his medicine. He looked at his father, who looked at the clock and waited explanations.

"Dad, I've done something awful."

He looked in vain for his mother who might have helped him out, he felt like a trapped rabbit.

His father's great shape loomed before him, "Come in Son, you're home now. You've no enemies here, no matter what you've done outside."

An arm went over the thin shoulders, it had been too long since that arm was there. So many times that great black monster had devoured good men and spewed nothing out but a hard empty shell for the family to live with. So many times Steve had yearned for the years when he had been young enough for his father to show affections ... it was not done now. Milestones had been reached which had been used to build up barriers between them, the hardness of the coal had seeped into the man. It was traditional, it was what coal did, it was a necessary state of mind. But some invisible thread was still there, it could still be used to pull the alarm bells if one of them tried hard enough.

Steve was home now, and it felt good.

Jobey was deep in thought, his mind sorely troubled. He would not get any sleep tonight as it was, without having this mystery to unravel. He took Margaret right to the gate. Now that he knew her parents knew all about him there was no point in hiding down the lane. They looked down to the pit-head where head-lights were still coming and going. No doubt Matty Wilson and the Bulldog were having a busy night.

They stood slightly apart as someone approached. It was Norman Booker, wearing plaster here and there, but not entirely unhappy.

"Come in, Jobey. Come in, man, and have a drink." Jobey looked at Margaret, who planted a quick kiss on her father's cheek and pushed Jobey through the gate. The parlour curtain moved slightly, Margaret alone noticed it; she hoped her mother was not going to be difficult.

"Leave your shovel out here, Jobey. What are you carrying that about for, anyway?" Norman Booker looked at Jobey with a puzzled stare.

"I'd like to see who this belongs to, if you don't mind Mr. Booker, I've got a special reason."

Booker lit the gas mantle and the room pop-popped into light. Mildred Booker came into the room and eyed Jobey up and down. He was covered in coal dust, clothes torn and dirty, and in his hands was a pit shovel which he was examining with care. She looked at the chintz-covered three piece suite and then at Jobey's disreputable appearance. Her eyes swept the room to the china cabinet with a lifetime's collection of exquisite pieces, to the Welsh dresser with it's assortment of hand-painted plates and figurines. There was so much furniture in the room there was only just enough room to move about, and here stood a giant of a man, waving a pit shovel.

She looked at her husband with a glance which dropped the temperature ten degrees. "Shall we go into the kitchen, Norman?" It was not a question but a command, and they trooped out of the parlour and along a passage to the kitchen. Margaret wrested the shovel from Jobey and flung it out of the door. For one awful moment she thought he was going to fetch it like some big faithful dog. She pushed him into the kitchen. "Get in there, Jobey. We've never had a shovel stolen from around here, yet. It will be there when you go. Mother, this is Jobey, I don't think you've met."

Jobey looked harassed, wiped his hands down his filthy trousers and took half a step forward, prepared to shake a hand, do a curtsey or go down on one knee. He grinned a trifle foolishly and awaited his cue.

"Hello, Job". Mildred's tone was strictly neutral.

"Hello, Mrs. Booker". Jobey bowed slightly from the waist, congratulating himself on thinking of that on the spur of the moment. "Sorry about the shovel, but we found it in the woods. Couple of chaps burying somebody. I thought it might have a name on it, but it doesn't. That means it's a Company shovel, Mr. Booker. Why should anybody be in the woods digging a grave with a Company shovel?"

All three leaned on the silence in the room and looked at Booker. He was involved in it, somehow. The longer the silence reigned the guiltier he looked. So much so, it was useless to deny anything. He had been caught out.

His eyes stopped flicking from side to side and his manner became calmer. "Welshman got killed today, that's all. Nothing to get dramatic about."

Mildred Booker recovered first. "Oh no, it doesn't matter. It was only a Welshman. Anyone can kill a Welshman if there's an 'R' in the month. What on earth are you involved in Norman, for God's sake?"

"It was an accident, that's all. The chap's got no relations. Friends either, if it comes to that. They're all going tomorrow, anyway. Quite frankly I didn't know what to do with him.

They wouldn't take the body, left it for me to deal with. Nothing to get steamed up about, accidents happen all the time."

"Dad, you know you can't do a thing like that. He must have some relatives at home."

"These chaps haven't got a home. They're the dregs of the valleys. Moving along like vultures to the next easy pickings. Your real Welsh miner wouldn't give them a kick up the arse."

Mildred advanced on her husband, "Norman, would it be an impertinent question to ask how many more you've had put down in that private wood. I mean, if you're mad enough to do it once, why not a dozen times?"

"Mother, don't be so dramatic. Perhaps it's not all that bad."

"Oh yes it is, and what's more we don't know the half of it." She glanced at Jobey, who swallowed and looked as apologetic as he could. Damned fool, why had he opened his mouth?

"Er, I think I'll be away then, Mrs. Booker. Thank you for asking me in."

"Jobey, don't go yet, please." Norman Booker took him by the arm. "You know, it's a lonely life, being Manager. There's nobody except your own family you can really trust. You have to build barriers all the time so people can call you names and it doesn't hurt. You learn to live on your own, I mean inside yourself where you're most vulnerable. If my family didn't care, I shouldn't want to go on. There's a point where nothing is worth it any more."

He had been through a long, hard day, and had clearly come to the end of his reserves. Jobey had never looked upon the Manager as anything but a sergeant-major. For the first time he saw through to the flesh and blood and the ragged nerves, and the weight of hundreds of lives pressing on his shoulders.

Jobey clasped the thin frame with his great hands, "We're with you, Mr. Booker. We've stood together already today and that's where we can stay."

He had no inhibitions when emotion came over him. With the impulsiveness of a child he said what he thought, and Jobey's thoughts were simple and positive, and always greatly to the benefit of somebody.

Mildred took Jobey by his arm. She raised her eyebrows at Margaret at the size and hardness of his muscles.

"Jobey, you're quite a character. You shame us all with your open heart and mind." She put her hands into her husband's. "Tell us about it some other time, Norman. When all this is over and you are good and ready."

Jobey took his leave with a very light heart. For the first time he began to wonder if he was going to marry Margaret. He had not dared to allow his thoughts to stray in that direction before, but her mother had called him Jobey. The word had not gone unnoticed by any of them.

He reached his home which was in darkness, and fumbled about behind the loose brick for the key, but could not find it. He tried the door, but it was locked, and he could tell by its rigidity that the bolt was also in place. Silly devil, locking the door. Probably the police patrols had scared the old man half to death. Jobey picked up a handful of slack and threw it at the window. The curtain moved, and he stood waiting for Pop to come down. After a few minutes he slung some more slack. This time the window went up on its sashcord with a squeal and a bang. Pop put his head out, "Clear off," he growled, his voice thick with stale beer and sleep.

"It's me, Jobey."

"I know who it is. Bugger off. You don't live here any more. Your clothes are in the lavatory."

Jobey looked at the door. He could burst through and go shake the old goat, and say "Who's been telling you things? I did what I'm paid for, and Booker's not as bad as you think he is." He noticed a movement in Matty Wilson's bedroom. Well, he wasn't giving him the pleasure of relating a family row, at the "Dog and Fox". Jobey turned without a word and walked away into the night. Not knowing or caring a deal, he went along Walker Street and sat on a front doorstep. So tired he could hardly see, he leaned back against the door and closed his eyes.

The front door opened quietly and he fell back in between somebody's legs. With a lightning reaction he chopped behind the knees and brought Rosie Button down on top of him, then stared at her in the gloom.

"What do you want to do that for, Rosie? Thought somebody was going to do me in then. I'll move on, out of your way."

She pulled him inside and into the kitchen. "Don't talk so daft, Jobey Rainbow. Everybody knows your Dad's locked you out because you stopped the men tonight. Where are you going to sleep then, and you looking like something the cat dragged in? You're not the only one not sleeping tonight, I saw you through the window."

"Why don't you get to bed, Rosie?"

"Bed? I've filled it so full of kids there's no room left for me." She sat him down on the sofa and poked the fire. "Put the raker on, really, but I can break it up." She jabbed at the large lump which would last all night with a shovel of slack behind it. She emptied the tea leaves onto the slack and put the big kettle to boil. The poker was returned to the large metal range where it hung with a rake, a toasting fork, and a button-hook for buttoning the boys' boots. "You had any tea, Jobey?"

"No, no Rosie, I'm not taking your food. Not likely."

She smiled at him from her soap-polished face. "I'm on your side, lad. I know what it's like to be lonely. We're two of a kind, you and me." He glanced round the kitchen which contained nothing but the barest essentials.

She spread the scrubbed table with a newspaper. "Sorry there's no cloth, but I wash it every Monday and we've only got the one. I always say nobody posh ever calls on a Monday, and now you've caught me out."

He smiled. "I'm not posh, Rosie. Just look at me." He was so tired he could hear his own voice as if it was a long way off. The ticking of the grandmother clock deadened his senses. He focussed his eyes on the rug on the hearth. It was worn in the middle, so Rosie had cut it in two and sewn the ends together to make a fresh middle. She was a real 'Nipcrust' was Rosie. She could make a good dinner from two pennorth of pot herbs and a few dumplings. The kids never went short.

The fire was warm. God! How tired he was. This day had lasted a week. He shuffled further into his clothes, feeling the warmth of his own body. Feeling fragile and unable to cope. Grateful for the shelter of this quiet room. Where was he going to sleep? Mustn't sleep here. Not right. Oh Rosie, he was so tired.

She swung his legs onto the sofa where Ted had slept many a week away. He hung over each end by quite a piece, so she used her only two chairs to prop him up. Fast on, he was like a great baby boy, his round face still betraying his innocent mind. She planted a slow kiss on his cheek which would make him dream of Margaret when the soundless hours had absorbed the deadly fatigue and tensions of his mind. Rosie's heart was big enough to add him to the family. He filled the whole place full of man. His straightforward and uncomplicated feelings found an echo in the goodness and mother-instinct she was blessed with. In this poor miner's kitchen, amidst the ashes and dust of the coal, lay the real story of the strike. Written in tears and the suffering of peopie desperately poor, but who were rich enough in spirit and hope to come back again when the bitterness had seeped away, absorbed back into the coal from which it came. Rosie curled up on the rug and blew out the candle, and night settled round them all, peaceful and restful, as night can be when people and passions have all gone to sleep.

* * *

Jobey woke the following morning to the full blast of Rosie's morning routine. A great saucepan of porridge was plopping on the hob. Big viscous bubbles slowly winked at him as he stared into the pan, wondering if his neck was really as stiff as it felt.

Thump! Thump! Thump! Oh hell, Rosie, stop that. She was thumping the ceiling with the copper-stick to waken the boys. The mutilated ceiling and the splayed out end of the bleached white stick bore evidence of the power of Rosie's arm. The loaves of bread had been cleared from the hearth to where the silver fish could not get at them. A great pile of thick slices of bread was on the table and Rosie had a basin of lard from which she scratched on a trace then scratched if off again. A thin sprinkling of sugar went on top, and breakfast was served.

An assortment of Coronation mugs and odd cups were set

out on the table, and Jobey's tea was poured into a basin. A most sensible arrangement, he thought. The boys went straight through to the back yard and washed under the cold water tap outside. Rosie had the upturned ponch tub alongside the tap, where it served as a soap dish and towel holder. She also used it as a table and scrubbed the vegetables out there, summer and winter.

The lads presented themselves for inspection, then came to the table. For towels they had sugar bags, well scrubbed and ponched. They were very coarse to the skin, but after the cold water they started the blood flowing again; according to Rosie.

Since Jobey and Rosie were using the only two chairs, the boys stood round the table to eat breakfast, eyeing Jobey with undisguised curiosity. They all knew him, and as nothing was volunteered to them as to why he was there, they all seemed to accept him. They gobbled back the food and went off with a clatter and the room seemed very quiet all of a sudden.

Jobey prepared to leave and met Minnie Varley coming through the door carrying a large thin book. She looked a little sheepish but smiled a warm smile at him. He thought of the unexpected squeeze of her hand at the funeral. He couldn't forget that. It had been a spontaneous warmhearted gesture such as Jobey knew and appreciated.

"Mrs. Varley," He squeezed her arm and leaned towards her confidentially. "Just returning the squeeze, Mrs. Varley."

"It's Minnie to you, young man. You make me feel ninety-two." He looked at the book. It was a child's reading manual.

"She's going to teach me to read, Jobey, if you must know." Rosie looked a little uncomfortable. "On my own now, you know. Got to make sure nobody twists me."

The two women went inside. Minnie Varley had never had much schooling but, as usual, she was willing to share what she had.

SEVEN

John Waverley told Booker to pay off the Welsh mercenaries and see that they went at once, he wanted the local men back. He thought they were about ready for work, and, as usual, he proved to be a pretty good judge of the situation.

Glyn Oliver, their leader, saw the chance to make a few bob on the side and went along to see Joe Bird, whose hackles rose at the sight of him. He looked at the 'foreign' blackleg with undisguised loathing, the Welshman was square and hairy. Joe didn't know whether to hit him and risk a good hiding or to just insult the creep. He pushed his face at the Welshman.

"Piss off." He put more venom into the words than there was in a viper. "You savvy English? You bloody mountain goat."

"Mr. Bird I ..."

"Back to your bloody caves, you blood-sucking vampires. We've nobbled you once and we'll do it again before you're much older."

"Mr. Bird, if we had the fare back home, we'd go. We know we're not welcome, but surely you wouldn't have us walking back to the Rhondda? You've got the funds, Mr. Bird. If you slip us ten bob each we'll walk it to Cardiff. I can't say fairer than that, now man. We'll be out of your way and nobody getting coal for the Waverleys."

It was quite a wonderful thought. Joe's biggest fear was that the solidarity of the men would break while there was work being done at the pit. The miners were on their own now that the General Strike was finished. This was a lock-out now, and Joe was beginning to sweat.

"How many of you?"

"Thirty-two, Mr. Bird. But some can't walk after the hiding we took at the pit. We'd have to get them to the station in a bus or a cart."

"Five pounds" said Joe Bird, "and not a penny more. I'll give it to you just before you get on the train. You're not coming any of your fly Welsh tricks with me, we're a cut too smart for you, round here."

Glyn Oliver looked a trifle disappointed, then brightened up. "Righto, Mr. Bird. It'll give us a bit of a start. My boys will accept your offer. Five pounds it is, payable this afternoon as we get on the train." He held out his hand to be shaken but Joe Bird spat on the palm. "We're paying to be rid of you, and that doesn't make us friends." The Welshman clenched a hairy fist, thought of his money and turned and walked away. They were going away in any case, the five pounds he was conning out of the Union man was just a bonus.

That afternoon about fifty miners stood around at Newthorpe station, watching the Welshmen with their brown paper parcels. A hoot in the distance and a ring on the bell heralded the arrival of the train. Oliver singled out Joe Bird and went for his money.

"We'll take our train fare, now, Mr. Bird. Kept our part of the bargain we have, I'm taking every last one of them with me."

Joe smiled at him for the first time and pushed a paper bag full of pig muck right into his face. At the same time a hose-pipe was turned on to the Welshmen and bags of soot and pig muck flew at them from all directions.

"You'll have to get up a bit bloody early to catch us, Glyn Oliver. I knew you were going, as soon as you did. Now get back to the land of how's-your-bloody-fathers."

Joe knew the miners in South Wales would have approved his attitude, for the Welsh miners in general were the most loyal in the country. The strike would never founder or even begin to crumble, in South Wales. They knew, there, how to tighten a belt, better than most.

Joe was very soon sobered up, however, by the sight that met him at the Donkey piece. The outcrops were all being opened up again. His crusade of the night before had proved very short-lived. His heart bled for them. Their main hope was to deny coal to the factories and houses, but they were pulling down their own defences by selling outcrop coal, and they were selling outcrop coal because they were losing their manhood and self-respect, as wives and children continued to suffer.

Notices began to appear all over the place, announcing a feast to be held in honour of Jud Palfreyman. It was to take place in the grounds of the church, and the Rev. Geoffrey Griffin would officiate. No-one was at all sure what it was about, but the significant phrase, standing out in bold black type for all to see was: 'A good meat tea to be provided for all'. It was the nineteen twenty-one bullock roasting all over again, and Joe Bird knew Waverley was playing his trump card.

When Saturday came round, the church grounds had never seen so much activity. A top table was laid for V.I.Ps and the rest had to manage by sitting on the grass, or squatting on their haunches in true collier fashion. A row of beer barrels stood behind the serving table, their great wooden bellies pregnant with good ale and as yet unborn evil intentions.

Jud Palfreyman sat in the middle of the V.I.Ps, a sickly grin plastered across his face, and Joe Bird hoped he might choke on a piece of fat ham. The Reverend Geoffrey started proceedings.

"Friends, I think I can call you friends."

That's a laugh for a start, thought Joe, everybody knew that over half the vicar's stipend came from the Waverleys. They resigned themselves to the tedium and fixed their eyes on the ham.

"Mr. Palfreyman is our representative on the free labour association, which, as you all know, has been formed to rescue men from the tyranny of the unions."

There was half a clap from here and there ... everybody had their eyes fixed firmly now on the boiled ham. Dobbin stood right over it, breathing in so deeply his taste buds started to drool. He had the look of a half-starved vagrant dog. Somehow he represented the degradation of them all, except that he lacked the veneer of dignity with which the others decently cloaked their appetites. Very shortly there would be handfuls of sweets tossed into the air for the children to fight over. There would be men with stomachs full to bursting who would wander into the nearest bushes to push their finger down their throats and so empty their stomachs to start again. It had been a hard long slog, and you always got the few who touched the depths.

Joe turned away from it all. From the human frailty, the hypocrisy the weapons of the 'Haves' and the Achilles heels of the 'Have Nots' which, at the moment, stretched all the way up to their slim bellies.

"The bastards", he muttered to himself. "Waverley, you'll answer for this."

* * *

Joe returned home a very thoughtful man. Every day it became harder to keep the men away from work, if Waverley made a crack in the wall it was more than possible the dam would burst. Morale had taken a dive since the T.U.C. had called off the General Strike.

Jobey also arrived home deep in thought. Looking next door he saw the Beggarlee Bulldog in Matty's doorway, sweat glistening on his forehead. He looked at Jobey uncertainly, then straightened his back. "Here, give us a hand, Jobey, got a patient being a bit difficult."

Jobey bent through the low doorway to see a pair of legs sticking out from behind the sofa. They were twitching spasmodically in a strange manner. Matty Wilson sat on the floor breathing heavily. He pointed to the legs. "Get him out, Jobey. We're trying to put his shoulder back but he won't co-operate." It was Sam Watson. As Jobey peered over the sofa he could see the drained look on the well-fed face. "Two hundred pounds in the Co-op", he thought, as he looked at Sam. The Bulldog and Matty would not give up until they had carved themselves a slice of that. Sam closed his eyes and let out a small sob as Matty took a good grip on the victim's hand and wrist. Matty then laid back on the floor and put one foot under the poor man's arm-pit and the other on his chest.

"Now then, Jobey, you hold him from sliding about", he gritted, tensing himself ready for the battle.

Jobey nodded his head, wondering what the Bulldog was going to contribute. Matty gave a sudden pull and the Bulldog sprang into action. He dropped beside Sam's head and clapped both hands over his mouth. It was bad publicity to have a lot of noise and shouting coming from the surgery.

The Bulldog's lips were moving silently. He looked into Jobey's eyes, "Say a little prayer to the Great Healer, Jobey." His eyes rolled upwards to the ceiling.

Jobey had a ridiculous urge to say "For what he is about to receive may the Lord make him truly thankful," He wanted to laugh; the wretched Sam was on the rack under his eyes, and he had a primitive desire to laugh at the poor man's agony.

Matty let go. He had pulled the shoulder back into place. He was not a man to quit easily.

A pained smile came on to Sam's face as he took off his cap, which had never left his head in the struggle. He took out two eggs and gave one to Matty and one to the Bulldog. "Here you are, boys. I know you don't charge a fee, but here is a reward for your labours." With that he was gone, swinging the arm slightly to make sure it was still all right.

Matty sat on the floor and looked at his sweaty egg. "The bastard, if he comes in here again I'll crucify him."

The Bulldog held up his hand. "The Lord accepted the widow's mite, just as we must accept Samuel's eggs. And that's why he's got two hundred pounds in the Co-op, the miserly sod."

Nothing more was said to Jobey, so he walked back into his own house. Pop was having gypsy toast for breakfast, a slice of bread thrown on the fire until it is burnt and blackened with soot. He claimed that he liked it that way. Neither of them spoke, but Jobey put the keys to the front and back doors in his pocket. He gave his father a look which was intended to intimidate him, but all he got back was an amused smile. Jobey was losing patience with the old man.

"You pile furniture against the door, and I'll throw you straight in the brook." He declared war.

"Honour thy father". Pop stood his ground and shouted the words. "Honour. What do you know of honour? All you honour is strength; and the Booker family. Hob-nobbing with people like that. They're only using you, can't you see that? As soon as this is over they'll drop you like a hot potato. Booker's making a right fool of you. Giving you fuchsias and dangling his daughter in front of your eyes. You've swallowed his bait all right, you have. Don't you know Ralph Waverley wants to marry her? What have you got to offer her except a bigger lump in your trousers?"

"You coarse old bugger. Don't you talk about my Margaret. I don't want her inside your mind. It's not a fit place."

"Think on, lad. Think on, before tha's made a laughing stock. And when tha's done with them, tha can come back here. I mean really come back. Until then this is only your home because of your size." He crammed the last piece of smoky toast into his mouth and Jobey could see tears in his eyes.

"Dad, Dad, I don't want to fight with you. Who have I got on my side, eh?" He took his father's shiny worn hands in his own.

"I just don't want to see you hurt, son. Can't you see they're a class above us? It can't be; ever. Tell yourself that, before you tear yourself apart with this silly dream. People are laughing at you. It doesn't want much to set them off, with you drawing pay while the family men are trying to manage on ten bob a week strike pay, and that's drying up any day now. Give it up, lad, give it up, and stop here where you belong."

"I can't, Dad. I love her and if I can't have her then I'm not bothered what happens. I live for her, nothing else in my life matters a brass farthing."

"Oh Jobey, you're young. You can get like this over another girl in time. I had lots before your mother. They're all bloody marvellous. God made us this way, so there'll be lots o' little Jobeys to carry on digging coal for the Waverleys."

Jobey stood up and pocketed his snap. "I worship her Dad. Take her away now and I'm finished."

He walked out of the house, dropping the keys on the table as he went.

His father watched him go. Many a young blood had used similar phrases, but he knew his Jobey. Pop shook his head, and the tears finally started to fall for his son. Strong as a bull, brave as a lion, vulnerable as a newborn baby.

"Jobey lad" he cried, "Your body's parted company with your brains."

EIGHT

The feast at the church was not an immediate success. The men listened to John Waverley and Norman Booker and then went away. It was still quiet at the pit, but Joe Bird knew a lot of seeds had been planted.

Pokey Jordan decided to make a quick killing with the outcropping before it came to an end. The lorries came from Nottingham twice a week to load up the precious coal, on Wednesdays and Fridays. It was Tuesday night when Pokey struck, having inveigled one of the drivers who was almost as big a rogue as himself; they began work at midnight, together with the ever present Sid Perkins. They toiled all night in the silent workings, loading up the lumps which had been stacked ready for the next day. About four-thirty, while Moorgreen was still fast asleep, the lorry pulled away, with Pokey and Sid peering out from the cab, ready to spring out and leave the driver to face the music if they were discovered. They were off to Nottingham to sell the coal.

The devil looked after his own, and they got away with it. Coming back from Nottingham they found a tramp asleep at Kimberley and stuffed a hedgehog down his trousers, just for the sheer joy of being alive with a pocketful of money.

Pokey went to bed in his pit dirt, trousers still on, with the money in his front pocket. You couldn't trust anybody, these days. They were in the "Dog and Fox" good and early, having gobbled back four quarts each before Tony Pandy came in. They were in fine form and greeted him like a long lost brother.

"Landlord, a pint of the best for one of the finest mountain sheep ever to leave Wales. We'll not ask why he left, eh?" Pokey's humour was as subtle as a battleship, and if times hadn't been quite so hard Tony would have told him what to do with his pint.

"You backed a winner, Pokey?" Tony Pandy put the question quite deliberately. There had been much speculation during the day as to where the coal had gone. It was obvious that these two had been drinking for some time, and money was deadly scarce now, even for men like Pokey who put themselves first.

"Yes. Cleaned up on a 'Donkey' as you might say." Pokey roared at his joke and Sid Perkins thought he had never heard anything quite so clever, so he added his bit to the humour. "Made right 'Donkeys' of 'em, didn't we?"

Tony glanced at Bill Swain the landlord. It looked very much as if Pokey was going to talk himself into a dip in the brook before the night was out. There was a stone bridge which went across the Erewash Brook at one end of the village. It was a drop of about twenty feet and the water was only about a foot deep at this spot. The bed was lined with large boulders and anyone thrown over the parapet was lucky to escape with no more than a broken leg. It was rough justice, but had been meted out several times when someone had offended against the community.

In spite of the free beer Tony had no love in his heart for Pokey, only Pokey loved Pokey. Tony pretended to leave. With a low cunning bred in him from many years of living rough, he knew Pokey wanted an audience and was willing to pay for it.

"Here, you're not going yet, Taff. Bill, give this bloody caveman a quart."

So it was a quart this time, Pokey was admitting his guilt every time he opened his mouth.

"I'll be with you in a second, Pokey. Shan't be a minute." He nipped outside to where he knew there was always a group of men who made this their meeting point. They all looked at the door to see who was lucky enough to have money to spare.

"Quick, one of you fetch Philip Burgin. Tell him I know who's pinched the coal." He sauntered back inside, wiping his hand down his trousers as if he had just cleared his nose between finger and thumb as was the custom with most of them.

Within thirty seconds there were faces casually looking in at the windows to see who Tony was accusing. A lot of them had lost coal, but Philip Burgin had lost most. He paid some of the men a daily wage to work for him and he sold their coal. This way men had some money to take home every day and didn't have to wait for payment from Nottingham. The men had been paid, and now there was no coal to sell. Philip Burgin was a hard man to cross and could rustle up a mob quicker than most.

"Where've you been, Taff? Your bladder's no bigger than a bloody egg. Swill this ale down you, there's plenty more where that came from. Get the bugger down you, Taff."

Philip Burgin came in rather over-casually, and Pokey swung his piggy eyes on to him then shut up like a clam. He knew that Burgin had owned most of the coal they had taken. He looked into his beer as if it contained some great secret of life, but Sid Perkins, who had drunk about his limit, had no reservations.

"We've swallowed about half a ton o' coal, eh Poke, eh? We'en swallowed enough beer to rot a bloody tree stump. Bill, give Burgin a drink wi' us. We've many a barrel to sup yet."

Pokey glared at Sid, but Sid was playing the big spender. "Have one yourself, Bill, have a quarten with me." He lifted his glass to them all, slapped a pound note on the bar and looked slowly round at the others to see their expressions.

All eyes were riveted on the pound note, and conversations froze unborn on their lips. All but Sid's. "Where's Martha? Never bloody here when a man's got money. I'll make her bloody stays rattle tonight. Come on, lads, let's sup some bloody ale." He picked up the pound note and put it down again to get the maximum effect. "Dusta sell bloody ale here, gaffer? Coal's money. Money's ale, i'nt it?"

Philip Burgin picked up the pound note. "I'll take care of this. It'll help pay for all that coal you've pinched."

Pokey managed to find some dignity to stand on. "You take that back, Burgin. No man calls me a thief."

"You're a thief and a liar, Pokey. I'm telling you this to your face. You're going over the bridge, Pokey, just as soon as a few friends of mine arrive."

At that moment the door was opened with a bang, and into the room strode about a dozen men. They had white silk scarves round their necks, folded over at the front and tucked under their waistcoats. Shiny navy-blue suits, lean as greyhounds, flat caps set square on their heads, and earnest, bony faces. Honest men, upright, law-abiding.

Pokey knew that the time for arguing was gone. These men had not come to accuse, but to carry out the sentence. He turned to Sid Perkins who was leaning at an exaggerated angle on the bar. "You great gormless tod. You're as thick as a brick shit-house", then he kicked Sid's legs from underneath him and bolted through the back door. Just for a few seconds Sid's recumbent body got in their way before he was trampled half to death as they all went over him. Pokey was built more for fighting than running and knew he was going to be run down if he trusted to his legs. He decided his only chance lay with the police, they were quick to break up any small gatherings. The nearest place was Martha's house, there were three billeted there, if he could make it.

He raced along the street, losing ground all the time, jumped her front wall and clawed at the door which had just slammed in his face. Martha had seen him coming. He heard the bolt sliding home and cursed her for a bitch and a whore. He was still cursing as he went over the bridge and hit the water flat on his back. His head hit a boulder which strained the tendons in the back of his neck, so that he walked with his head down for the rest of his life. There were some who said his affliction was only to be expected. The Bulldog said "The Lord works in a mysterious way." Most agreed with his word but not with his delivery, he always gave the impression that he was in the Lord's confidence, and one suspected that if a difference of opinion arose the Bulldog would win, or start a splinter group.

* * *

Jobey was calling on Margaret every night now. Their favourite spot was Misk Hills where the September air was surely richer than anywhere else on earth. They toiled their way through the great clumps of blackberry brambles to the top of the hills, whilst Margaret's conversation washed the coal dust out of his mind. Here they could push waist high through the russet and gold, and watch startled hares peer inquisitively over the bracken and ferns. On the high moorland there was a tranquil balm to leaven the air ... it was Sunday every day.

"We'll just sit on this stile, Jobey, and listen to what the birds are talking about."

He sat on the bottom step with his head on her knees, eager for the sound of her voice.

She put her soft hand inside his shirt, casually, almost absently tracing a smooth finger along the line of his ribs. Jobey shuddered and looked up. She could see he was miles away, he was watching the clouds, so sharply etched against the blue of the sky they were almost tangible objects. Fleeting visitors from over the hill, they moved on – to where the grass was ever greener. The coal could not blacken them, they were free. They were not tainted with gossip; with winning and losing; with man-made right and wrong. Neither was Jobey really. He had an affinity with their ponderous woolly ways, with their boldness and big obvious outlines.

He stroked her thighs and she knew he had switched from clouds to another subject which was dear to his heart.

She gave him a smile but remained perfectly still as he fumbled at her in the bright sunlight of an Autumn afternoon. He rolled her into the long grass and bracken where she lay on her back, the clouds could almost be touched from here. She was strangely detached.

Jobey went from clouds to the soft warm intimacy of his rough lovemaking. But what was in between ... A nearby sycamore was turning its large floppy leaves in the breeze, exposing their soft pale underbellies to the harsh light and hardening elements.

"You'll never see the sun set behind the sycamores," her mother had said. "It will just disappear behind the slag hills, suddenly, cruelly."

Jobey was above her, blotting out the sunlight, and she was not responding. He took time off from his urgent preoccupation to look into her eyes in puzzlement.

"Not now, Jobey".

"Darling ...?"

She could see the awful rejection which registered in his face and it struck at her heart, but he had to learn.

"Jobey. A girl doesn't always feel like it."

"Why not?"

He was blunt and unsubtle as a prize bull. Oh God – she fumbled in her mind for the strength for both of them.

She lay there almost naked in a world of thorns and sharp stones – and began to have doubts but had no time to consider them. Jobey was hurt, she had wounded the great massive bulk of him because she possessed weapons he could never know about. There were a million things Jobey would never know about if they were to make a life together. She dismissed them for now and wrapped her legs round him. It was no time for talking.

They had no need for words, they had Misk Hills in the Autumn, they had each other and a young inquisitive love. It took them a million miles from Moorgreen and the agonies of mind which the men were enduring.

* * *

Tater Varley decided to go back to work. It was nothing to do with Minnie, who made it her business to make no overtures at all. Her man would go back when it was right for him to do so. Jobey saw him coming and put himself in Tater's path, ready to speak to him. Tater went right by without so much as a nod of the head and Jobey's stare followed him like a little boy who nobody wanted to play with. None of the men spoke to him or acknowledged his existence. The bluff good humour which characterised their end-of-shift behaviour seemed to freeze if he was around. Jobey had hoped that the first men back at work would be on his side, sort of workers against non-workers, but it was not to be. There were few of them who had not seen Jobey standing on the truck, denying the men access to the drift at Westwood. They had not stoned him, but neither had they forgiven him. They accepted his protection but that was as far as it went.

Tater held his head high and looked straight ahead. He was on his own, and his pit boots rattled on the road as he hastened along, hoping to beat the dawn chorus, led by Mrs. Frogson.

She was there, as usual. There were about fifty men back at work now and she accompanied each one or group of them along the road, beating a frying pan with a spoon. Tater kept to the middle of the road because if he travelled near enough to the houses someone would empty their 'slops' over him.

Red hot ashes were poked out of all the fires along Engine Lane and flung into the road as the men went by. Tater's studded boots ignored the hot coal, but his nose took up the acrid smell of burning dust and passed it on to his brain where it burned with a slow sullen awareness that he was hated by his fellow creatures, the only creatures he knew. Many people were born and passed their whole life-time within five miles of the same spot. They died and were buried, without any desire to know what lay over the other side of the hill. To be ostracised by this close-knit tribal community was a frightening experience for them.

Mrs. Wharmby threw a dustpan full of bedroom sweepings over her gate just as he was about to pass. "Well, well. Sorry I'm sure, Mr. Varley, I didn't expect anyone going to work. Sorry about that, I'll be more careful tomorrow."

Tater was not a man to stand on ceremony. He walked back to Florrie Wharmby's house to catch her. She saw him coming and shouted to her husband, who was still in bed.

"Alf, Alf. Get up, you idle swine. Tater Varley's after me." She swung her fat hips along, too fat to run. Tater grabbed her by the hair and poured his quart bottle of water all over her.

"Get back to bed, you great bag of lard," he shouted. Alf Wharmby did not get up until mid-day. Alf was enjoying the strike, and if his Missus chose to get into a running fight with the scabs, well, that was her business.

Mrs. Frogson was following ten yards behind. Tater ground his teeth. Really there was nothing a man could do about this, without losing his dignity. Suddenly there was an extra loud thump and Mrs. Frogson screamed. She collapsed in a heap as Minnie Varley brought her own frying pan into play, a heavy iron one which had been in the family for years.

"It's had many a pound of bacon, but never a pig's head in it before," she called. Several other women who were part of Mrs. Frogson's band set on to Minnie. They pulled her hair until she screamed, turned her on her back and soaked her in slops. She was full of spirit, but there were too many of them.

Tater hastened on his way. He would make sure she did not follow him again. Minnie Varley was one of the best known and best liked women in the village, trusted with the money for Christmas Clubs and Clothing Cards. He knew she would take it hard, but he also knew that the women who had attacked his wife had pawned just about everything except their wedding rings, had seen their children play all day without shoes, and had seen the look in their man's eyes as each Friday night came and went without wages.

Bert Honey had been pulled from his bed and beaten up in his own house for daring to be the first man to go to work. His wife had fetched Jobey Rainbow, but it had been too late. There were some who said she had taken a 'short cut' via Philip Burgin's house and spent half an hour there. It could well be true. Ada Honey had nothing to thank Bert for these past fifteen years.

Tater knew all this, he knew that many years must pass to soak up all the bitterness. The pit was like a boil on the pleasant landscape and the great black hole was a suppurating tide of poison which filled every man's soul and overflowed into the women and children. That's why he smiled a great smile and silently shook hands with himself at the sight of Charlie Wildgoose waiting at the crossing which led to the pit. Now they would show them how to get coal. The old team of Tater and Charlie. They seemed to strike sparks off each other. No back-slapping, no flamboyant greetings, just a life-time of quiet respect and sober regard for each other. Tater slowed down to let Charlie fall into step, but Charlie didn't do so. Tater turned with a smile which fell away from the corners of his mouth at the sight of a stream of tobacco juice from Charlie. The saliva was expertly directed; right across Tater's boots. He turned to leave a very sad and lonely Tater Varley. Life-long friendships ripped apart and ground into the coal dust that gave them birth. There was truly a vicious monster now in their midst.

Word has passed along that two thousand colliers were marching from Yorkshire. They did not like the sound of pits in the Midland with more men at work than there were locked out. Unfortunately a lot of the Yorkshiremen were not typical miners but men who went along for the pickings a mob can get. The first night they slept around a farm. Newly made haystacks were pulled to bits and used for bedding. Turnips were eaten raw for breakfast, so that the fields appeared to have been visited by a swarm of locusts. The police ignored the whole procession, keeping a diplomatic distance so long as the miners stuck to turnips. Somebody was going to have trouble but that could be tomorrow, when they got to Eastwood.

The unruly mob went along like a column of soldier ants. Any food which got in their way was devoured and left behind in filthy hedge-bottoms. They could strip an orchard in ten minutes and kick in the teeth of any guard dog which tried to stop them. They ate the lot. Stalk, pips and any resident grubs in the apples.

John Waverley had not been a Colonel for nothing. He had fifty policemen surround the pit-head, and Norman Booker and Jobey decided to sleep in the lamp-house until the Yorkshire tykes had been turned. The tension grew and rumours came to the pit every hour.

A platoon of infantry had shot the leaders at Annesley, and the rest had fled in disorder.

They had been joined by another two thousand men from Mansfield and martial law had been declared.

They were evicting farmers from their homes and slaughtering cattle and sheep.

The most outrageous rumours were given credence and passed on to wide-eyed listeners for the tale to snowball as it travelled.

The truth was that the march was losing impetus all the time. The local population gave them no help at all. It was as if even the most ardent strikers were determined to keep it in the family. They resented the foreigners from the North who were interfering in a private fight. The police grew bolder and took away about twenty hardy spirits who had forcibly taken over a pub and drunk it dry. They were leathered good and hard about the head by the police who hit them with their capes. None of the marchers complained. These were violent times and corporal punishment was the order of the day. The kids lined the road-sides chanting "Yorkshire born and Yorkshire bred, strong i'th arm and weak i'th head." Even the weather turned against them. By the time they reached Eastwood there were only about two hundred of them still in the column. The police opened up the Eastwood Empire for them to sleep in for the night and generally disarmed them by friendly behaviour. It takes two to make a fight. They really looked a sorry sight now they had walked the violence out of themselves. Poor thin suits, soaking wet through, showing the sharpness of their knees and elbows; some mothers' sons who had been too long without a square meal.

John Waverley opened up his coffers and had them all provided with a bellyful of sheeps-head soup and a basinful of rice pudding. They bound up their shoes with strips of cloth and set off back for home, with a general impression that the Nottingham area was not too bad at all, really.

When the last of them departed, John Waverley gave the signal for retreat, and the waiting battalion sheathed their bayonets and emerged from Watnall Woods where they had been deployed for the last three days. If an ex-Colonel couldn't get a bit of protection, it was a poor show.

The failure of the Yorkshire Marchers seemed to stimulate the return to work of a lot of the waverers. Every day the number grew until there were more men at work than there were out. The Geordies and South Wales were still solidly out.

There was safety in numbers and a lot of people from out of the district began to arrive at the Utopian Midlands, where a man could actually work and draw a pay packet. At Moorgreen the pit was filling up rapidly, and the staunch strikers who would not give in began to realise that their places were being filled by total strangers.

All the ponies were now back down the pit, and this was a bad omen. They were strictly neutral, and the fact that their presence was required below ground was a mute admission that all was right wwith John Waverley's world. Their eyes were focussed now for their other world, and the miners must do the same. Nystagmus, the disease of the eyes caused by inadequate lighting, again returned to bedevil the unfortunate colliers. Dr. Alexander said fifty percent of them suffered from this disease to some extent. None of the men called it nystagmus, it affected the eyes so it was 'eye-stagnus' to the men who had it.

Florrie Wharmby had a go at Alf. The novelty of beating pans had worn off, and there were too many at work now, and she had never really been happy on the same side as that common Mrs. Frogson, and having a pay packet was better than beating pans any day. She left it until Alf was in a good mood. He had just got rid of Aunt Ethel by putting the "Raker" on. This was a large lump of coal which lasted through the night, and Alf had a subtle way of packing off unwelcome guests with it. He made a great show of putting the lump carefully in place and packing dead slack behind it, then the teapot was emptied onto it to the accompaniment of much hissing and spitting from the fire.

This clearly meant "Well, I don't know about you lot, but I'm off to bed." Of course it worked, and Aunt Ethel left in a huff. Florrie was not too pleased, as Ethel was seventy-six if she was a day, and had no family of her own.

She pulled the tin bath onto the hearth and filled it up from the boiler and the big kettle. Alf settled in with a contented sigh, and Florrie struck.

"Lot of men back now, Alf. There'll be no jobs at all soon for them as stops out much longer."

Alf had been expecting this. He was small, but round and jolly. He weighed fourteen stone, according to the Gypsy Queen at Moorgreen Show. It had been a good two pennorth really, she had pressed and squeezed him all over before announcing her guess. He had wobbled his stomach for her and they had all had a good laugh. Alf could set his protruding stomach on the wobble so that it resembled a giant blancmange doing a rhumba. Alf could laugh with anybody. At five-feet-five you didn't get to be fourteen stone by whittling about what might happen.

"Now Florrie, my old duck, tha mustna interfere in things tha' doesn't understand." Alf looked wise and dipped his pot dog into the water. It was hollow and just right for filling with water and pouring all over his back. The water came out at just the right speed, better than a fancy sponge. He had won it three years ago at Nottingham Goose Fair. It was highly glazed in a hideous orange colour, but it was Alf's pride and joy. It was the only thing he had ever won, so it stood on the mantle-shelf and had about four baths a year.

"Alf, it's all right having principles when you can afford it. Principles don't fill empty bellies."

"Now shut up, me old bod. Dunna whittle."

"But Alf, every morning now I can hear all them men going to work. You listen in the morning."

"Now I'll ask thee summat, my old darling. Can ta hear any women among 'em?"

"You know as well as I do, what I mean. There's only them that's a bit slow or idle that's still stopping out."

Alf stood up in the bath, water cascading off his soapy belly, ready to protest.

Florrie beat him to it. "For God's sake get some clothes on. You don't have a bath very often, but it puts me off you for a fortnight when I see you like that. Your belly's that hard I could crack a flea on it."

Now this was getting personal and Alf had to strike back. Being the sort of shape he was, Alf had schooled himself to take it out on inanimate objects whenever possible. He picked up the poker and slopped his way to the fire and gave the raker a good crack. A shower of sparks emitted and, worse still, a few hot cinders shot out. Alf trod on one which wedged between his toes.

"Bloody hell. Bloody hell." At last he got rid of the hot cinder and sat on the squab, nursing his injuries and using some proper pit language.

"Are you all right Alf?" Florrie thought she ought to ask. He jumped up, picked up his bowler hat off its peg behind the door, flung it on the floor and kicked it as hard as he could. It flew across the room, knocking over a jug of milk which went all over the cat.

"Now are you bloody satisfied?" He glared at Florrie, who decided that the precious moment had gone and Alf was not yet ready to forsake his principles.

Florrie Wharmby had been right about one thing, the jobs were being filled, often by men who wanted work at any price. A lot of the houses had "knocking up" times chalked on the wall. The knocker-up then came along with his long pole with wires stuck in the end. These he rattled on the bedroom window and didn't stop until he was given a signal from inside.

The Paddy started to run regularly again. This was a primitive railway engine, with even more primitive carriages, which carried the miners to the pit-head from the surrounding villages. Philip Burgin used to catch this. Always a man with one eye on the cash, he had abandoned his outcropping for the longer term outlook of keeping on the right side of Norman Booker.

The Paddy was his pet hate. It made him feel something less than human. It was standing in now, with Desmond Wooten, the driver, making it hiss, so that the noise was going to take all day to die down in his ears. He took the single high step which brought him into the carriage, into the stink of second-hand coal dust, wet clothes, sweaty men and an undefinable smoke-steam combination. Six o'clock came and it pulled out. Zombies packed like sardines, bound for the communal grave. The men spoke in grunts, if at all. This was necessity in the raw.

The Paddy swayed and rattled, taking its cold, lonely cargo to the private world below ground. A terribly small world, bounded by the limits of a man's inadequate lamp. All beyond it had died. Every small thing which made life tolerable was gone, behind the thick black wall. Perhaps he would pick up the threads again when he had wished another piece of his life away; when this monster had wrung him dry of his life force, drained him of every reserve that food and sleep and nature provided. Then he would be out, and left to his own devices for a few precious hours, knowing that he had a date the next day with the monster. All this, and much more the Paddy meant to Philip Burgin.

The Paddy rattled crazily on through the dark September morning. The only mellow fruitfulness about this particular piece of morning was the language. Almost as if the crude utterances were a measure of each speaker's manliness, any statement volunteered started with a built-in accusation against the speaker, because he had not kept his mouth shut like the rest of them. The swearing was by way of being an apology for disturbing the numbness of mind which helped to cushion the crude early morning world they had to endure.

In the village the bitterness overflowed until no family in the district was not being pulled apart in some way. The men returning to work had to take whatever conditions were handed out; no bargaining allowed, no protection given. The Federation were not interested in anyone who was at work.

House-to-house canvassing was laid on by Norman Booker in a final attempt to beat Joe Bird and his officials. Deputies who were back at work took men still out to the pubs, and filled them to the brim with good ale and advice. The miner, being a friendly, reciprocating person by nature, often responded by turning up for work. Norman Booker was winning now, the breach in the wall was wide and deep. Joe Bird searched his conscience as very few men have had to do before him. If he appealed to the brave spirits who were still out to stay out with him, their jobs would be filled perhaps forever, by strangers. They would become known as the hard core of dissenters and trouble-makers, their reward for being steadfast was poverty. The men's natural instinct to protect their families was put on the scales against their life-time's abhorrence of the blackleg.

Joe turned the matter over and over in his mind. Oh God, what should he ask of these men? The desperate struggle was being lost. It was almost over in his district. They were the diamond-tip on the tool which the Owners and the Government had used very deliberately in Nottinghamshire to break through the protective wall of solidarity which was the miners' only hope.

He could not ask the men to take any more. He thought of Norman Booker's words "Are you going to wait for suicides? You can lead them Bird, nobody else." His head throbbed, and he felt numb as he forced himself to acknowledge the truth of Booker's statements. "You can't win ... The Government's taken you on ... You can't win, can't win ... It's all over, all over." He shattered himself by repeating the thought, time and again until he could live with it, and so he made his fateful decision to go to Norman Booker and negotiate a deal of sorts. It didn't amount to much, and to a lot of people in other parts of the country it looked like total capitulation. He had, of course, signed his own death warrant.

His vision at Hucknall had proved all too true. The Owners had chosen the battleground and the time of the battle, they knew the mood of the Government. The Federation had been ill-advised to start a confrontation at this time of year, and with so little money in the kitty.

He would be remembered by Owners as the Ringleader in

his district. He would be remembered by the Federation as the arch-enemy ... the first official to break the solidarity and advise his branch to go back to work. He would be remembered by the men as the big name in their slide to poverty and humiliation, and as it is in the nature of things to blame somebody, his name would be synonymous with the degradation and bitterness that went with defeat. He could salvage nothing but his own self-respect. Unfortunately that didn't pay the rent.

The only consolation Joe Bird had was that one day another generation must spring up who would learn from these mistakes, but their time had not yet come.

Other areas of the country now began to accept the inevitable. Slight 'Face-savers' were put forward for the Federation to talk about, but the men had to accept the Owners' terms.

Meanwhile the scapegoat stuck out like a sore thumb – Joe Bird was due for the chop.

NINE

There was no Christmas spirit in the coal industry now the lock-out was finished. Shovels were outlawed, and if any man sent up a tub of coal with too much slack in it he received no pay at all for any of the coal in that particular truck. Petty officials who had the 'Gaffer's Ear' were tin gods. When setting on workers, preference was given to men with boys in the family, since they were a potential source of cheap labour.

Some of the popular press commiserated with the miners, but that didn't pay the bills.

The men were helpless to hit back. There was no money in the kitty and no heart left in them, and now an example must be made. So it was that no-one was less surprised than Joe Bird when he was told not to turn up for work again.

It was December the twenty-first, and Norman Booker sent for Jobey to come to his Office. He had to push through half a dozen unsavoury characters who were milling round the Manager's door looking for a throat to cut. A long queue of men waited respectfully along a passage. Booker might or might not get around to seeing them today, if not, no matter. They would come again the next day, and the next; take some of the cockiness out of them.

"Sit down, Jobey." The Manager swung round in his teak swivel chair and indicated an upright hard wooden seat against the wall. "Got a job for you today. Sort of Christmas Box for Joe Bird."

Jobey looked puzzled. "Heard he's got the sack, Mr. Booker. What do you want with him?"

"Exactly, Jobey, exactly, living in a Company house too. Not right, that. All the Company houses are required for employees. Can't have non-Company men in them. I want him out, Jobey." He flung a fold of papers on to the desk. "Call at the Police Station, you'll find a bailiff waiting for you.

Here's the necessary authority by the law. I've sent for a few men from outside the district, they're waiting for you outside my door, take them with you, they stink to high heaven."

Booker turned to his desk and picked up the telephone. Jobey looked at him with open mouth. A big calendar was pinned to the wall with the dates crossed off as though a prisoner were counting the days of his sentence. December the twenty-first. The season of goodwill to all men was just about here.

Outside in the darkening afternoon he could hear the male voice choir practising carols in the first-aid room. He could picture the scene at Joe Bird's.

Joe was a marked man. No-one dare give him work. All the local businesses depended on the colliery in some way or other. Emma Bird would manage. She made jam out of rhubarb and everything. She could make do for three days on a sheep's head. No-one could cook a sheep's brains quite like Emma, they stood up on the plate, fit for a king. But she was worried right now. They were proud, were Joe and Emma. They held their heads a bit higher than most. Now he had to take this pack of scum along and say, "Joe, I've brought a few friends and we're going to put your bits and pieces out in the street. Everything you own is to be spread out in the snow of this dark December evening. People will be sorry, and curse the Owners and Management, but they will curse from the solid comfort of a home."

Jobey stared hard at the floor, then raised his eyes to the Manager, who picked up the sheaf of papers and tossed them to him.

"Get cracking, Jobey. Those animals outside will give the place a bad name. I want him out today, not tomorrow."

Jobey stood his great height alongside the Manager's desk. Very firmly he took the telephone out of his hand and returned it to the rest. Jobey was angry. Once, about every five years or so, Jobey got really steamed up about something. When this happened his vocabulary couldn't cope, so he made do with what he had.

"You bloody pig!"

Booker looked startled, "Eh?"

"You bloody black pig." Jobey breathed the words down

his nose and searched the Manager's face for a physical likeness to Margaret. How could they be father and daughter and yet live in two such different worlds? "Take your foul scum, and deliver the papers yourself."

"Now look here, Rainbow. Whose side do you think you're on? There's such a thing as knowing which side your bread's buttered. You're not indispensable, you know."

"I'm not living in a Company bloody house, you can't turn me out for Christmas."

Someone came to the door. "Get out," roared Booker. The door shut again quickly. The phone started to ring and Jobey picked it up and threw it on the floor. Booker looked scared now, he thought Jobey was about to attack him.

"If you touch me I'll forbid Margaret ever to see you again. You'll not work for the next fifty years. I'll see to that, personally."

"I'm not going to touch you, you're Margaret's father, but she'll make up her own mind about me, and if you want Joe Bird's head you're going to have to get it yourself. Never mind who's side I'm on, Joe Bird fought for us all. He's been slung out of the Federation, lost his job, and now his house. Where's he going to live?"

"Live?" Booker leaned forward towards Jobey. "He could live in jail for the next twenty years if I brought up certain charges. Let him go to the Forty Bridges. He'll know what time of day it is there, when the trains go over. Bed down with his Communist pal Rhondda Valley or whatever his name is."

"Tony Pandy" said Jobey automatically. He was calming down now. "Look, Mr. Booker, will you forget this for my sake?"

"For the last time, Jobey, are you going or not? Bird is getting out of his Company house today. If I send these lads outside here, they'll throw his stuff out of the bedroom window, and enjoy doing it. You may be able to keep them under control. Now what's it to be?"

Jobey hung his head. Always a practical thinker, he realised the truth of what Booker had said. Joe Bird was sure to have a go at them and they would enjoy working him over. Also he didn't like the reference to twenty years' jail for Joe. He thought it was probably too late now for Booker to bring charges, but ... He picked up the papers and walked out slowly. He took the motley bunch with him, and they stood outside Joe Bird's house while the bailiff delivered the papers.

A crowd quickly gathered as the word spread up the street. The bailiff had brought two policemen with him, both newcomers to the district. The only enemy the crowd could identify was Jobey. He had been on the side of the bosses all along. The merciless turning of the screw that had taken place these last few weeks had worked them all into a frenzy of hate, and things began to look bad.

As the crowd grew bigger it also grew bolder, until with a sudden rush they attacked Jobey and his small band. The miners were hard and physically strong, and used feet as well as fists. However, the imported thugs whom Norman Booker had called in were no sluggards at dishing it out. They had had more fights than hot dinners, and the snow was soon stained with blood. Even the lamp-lighter joined in with his pole.

Jobey pushed into the house and closed the door behind him. The front room was bare, as he leaned with his back to the door, looking at what had been a home. A Chinese lantern of cheap paper hung from the ceiling. A badly made paper chain hung from the wall, doubtless a present from one of the youngsters next door. The place was cheerless, and matched his mood.

The commotion raged outside and he knew he was funking his duty. His heart was not in it, he couldn't bring himself to fight against Joe Bird's neighbours. He just hadn't the stomach to fight anybody any more. How had he got himself into this mess? What nightmare had he weaved for himself, and how long was it going to last? His life had turned into a series of upsets, joined together by bitter silences. It was eating into Jobey's sensitive soul, he just could not go on.

Joe Bird came through the doorway and saw the agony on Jobey's face. Jobey shook his head, his throat was a hard dry lump, and Joe knew it.

"Don't trouble yourself, Jobey, this is not your doing. You're caught in your net like I'm caught in mine. We're very small fish. I shall have to go, whether you help or hinder, it doesn't matter." He took Jobey's arm and opened the front door to see feet and fists flying. At the sight of Joe Bird and Jobey standing together, the men stood quite still. Joe let them stew for a few seconds before he spoke.

"Gentlemen, I thank you. When all else fails we have our two strong arms and those of our friends, but this is useless. We cannot fight the might of the British Law. When you have spilled good blood into the snow I shall still have to go. Jobey Rainbow is our friend. He has been a good friend throughout the strike, and I wish you all to know that." He took Jobey a few steps further. "Now friends, if you wish to help me, will you please help carry this stuff to my son's house, where we shall be staying for Christmas. Can't beat having kids around at Christmas, it's an ill wind that blows no good. And remember what the Bulldog says, "Whomsoever the Lord loveth, He chasteneth!" My God, he thought to himself, if the Lord hadn't said that, we'd have had to invent it.

Joe had known that the inevitable next step to his sacking would be eviction. Somebody had to be made an example of, and who better than the man who had led them all? Had the bailiff left it one more day he would have found an empty house.

The Company men followed Jobey back to the pit, where he left them to squeeze as much as they could out of Norman Booker. He took his lamp and his tag and handed them in, then went to the Manager's Office. Booker was putting some papers in a safe when Jobey walked in.

"You don't need me any more, Mr. Booker, I shall not turn up for work again, I've finished with the job. You'll be pleased to hear that, I'm sure. I suppose I was never cut out to be a Gaffer's man." With that, he quietly closed the door and was gone.

Norman Booker smiled to himself, and did a little dance. Two birds with one stone, just as he expected. What a good day's work this was. Doctor Alexander would have to find a new guinea pig, which was a pity, he was ready to start work again and nobody knew the old workings like Jobey. Still, a small price to pay, better to keep the Doctor out of the way for a while, anyway. Moorgreen was turning into a very fiery pit, just lately. Gas was cropping up all the time, and the best way to deal with gas was to keep working. Once the workaday rhythm was lost by pulling men out, the gas tended to collect in pockets and cause all sorts of trouble.

Dr. Alex was good propaganda. Humane, clever, trusted by all the men, but inclined to be over-cautious. Technically brilliant, but academic in his approach, lacking the hard-line solution which pit Managers had to adopt. It was one long compromise between going by the book and taking calculated risks. It was all right for the Doctor, his head was not on the chopping block if production was down. In any case, the major cause of accidents was roof falls, and gas had nothing to do with that – as a rule.

The Doctor was not always right. He had persuaded Booker to use some steel props instead of wooden ones. They were stronger all right, no doubt about that. The trouble was they held until the pressure from the roof made them spring out like arrows from a bow, and then the roof went, and it was too late. With a wooden prop there would be creaking and splintering first, giving an experienced miner a few seconds warning to be out of the way before the roof came down.

Booker rubbed his hands again. This was his day, he could hardly wait to get home and tell Mildred that Jobey Rainbow was out of a job. She was putting the pressure on Margaret a bit now, and Ralph Waverley was calling tonight with something special – a gold watch for Christmas. Let Jobey Rainbow match that; out-of-work miner. If young Waverley played his cards right, and Mildred put on a bit more pressure, this could be the break-through they had been looking for. Rainbow could go take a jump into Moorgreen Reservoir. The lock-out was over. He was expendable.

The phone on his desk went again, and Seth Sloman his Under-Manager got the surprise of his life; Norman Booker answered in a sweet reasonable voice, "Booker here, what can I do for you?"

Sloman looked at his receiver as if not believing his ears ... Jacob Marley's ghost must have visited Booker and worked a transformation.

"It's the gas readings again, Norman. In 66 districts it stands at three percent, now."

Three percent! Booker whistled to himself.

"The Mines Inspector's not due yet."

Sloman grunted loudly.

"What's that Seth?"

Sloman grunted again, cleared his throat, then spoke:

"He's got to come sometime, hasn't he? I mean, the readings are all here in the book."

"I'll talk to him when he does come."

"I've got a very unhappy fireman down here Norman. I mean, I can't tell a fireman there's nothing wrong, he'll soon tell me where to go – and he's real unhappy."

"The world is full of unhappy people Seth. It's 'Bull' week isn't it? They're all trying to make a bit extra for Christmas."

"Yes," Sloman sounded very uncertain, then added: "The temperature's up – so's the barometer, come to that."

These were ominous signs.

Booker was riding high today, however. "The best way to deal with it is to keep working, Seth. There's a two-day break coming for Christmas, the place will be solid with gas if we don't keep going now."

There was a pause from Sloman's end.

"O.K. Seth?"

"If you say so, Norman."

"I do. I do. Cheers for now." He put the phone down. He didn't want to hear any more. There'd be the devil to pay when the Inspector called. Oh well, a few more years of this and he'd be retiring, let young Sloman have all the headaches.

Three percent gas. He would have to speak seriously to Waverley about this gas. Dr. Alex would be furious too, when he saw the readings. After Christmas he was starting down the pit again, with or without Jobey Rainbow.

* * *

Jobey did not call at Booker's house that night, he was afraid of the reception he might get. He hung around the lane, knowing that Margaret could see him from her window. He looked rather shaggy and ill-kempt against the porcelain landscape. Somehow he didn't belong in the lane with its exquisitely shaped columns and spires of sparkling white crystal. He was dark, intruding and faintly disturbing. It was quite a long time before she eventually went out to him, and they sauntered off down the lane, putting their feet carefully into the cart-tracks which cut into the frozen snow like the knife scores on a leg of pork.

"I suppose your Dad told you that I've talked myself out of a job today. I'm not going to apologise, Margaret, I'm not cut out for the sort of work he wanted me to do."

"That's all right, Jobey. My Dad's got his troubles, we've got ours." Her tone was a little flat, none of the musical enthusiasm her voice had always carried. He sensed immediately that something was wrong. He picked up and echoed her every mood. His love projected into her aura like a sensitive antennae.

"We've got our troubles?" His own voice sounded rather small and hesitant. He didn't want this conversation to go on. He shouldn't have come tonight.

They stopped against a five-barred gate which the frozen snow had decorated with thick layers of icing sugar. Jobey aimed a kick to shake off the snow, but it didn't move. "Frozen hard," he said, in an effort to sound matter-of-fact and change the conversation. She didn't answer, just stared hard into the valley below, where the night workers had just started their long, quiet stint.

Jobey felt for her hand, "I'll get another job, Margaret, you'll see. I'll go and see Mr. Noon tomorrow. I know he'll fix me up, always told me to go and see him if ever I wanted a job. Mr. Noon's a very good friend of mine, says I'm the only one who can handle that boar of his. It's vicious, you know, sliced Henry Millership's leg open last week. I can handle him though, Mr. Noon knows that."

Margaret knew that neither Mr. Noon nor anyone else would offer Jobey any gainful employment, now. He had turned his back on the only 'Friends' he had, today. She turned her wrist to look at the new gold watch which Ralph Waverley had presented to her at tea-time.

"Jobey, I want to go home. I'm not thinking very clearly."

"Margaret," he put an arm round her.

"No, Jobey don't let's talk. Just take me home. There's an awfully cold wind across these fields." She pulled away and started back up the wheel-ruts, carefully picking the safe spots to tread on.

He walked alongside her, treading in the deep snow so that he could put out a helping hand for her to lean on. Only the crunching and squeaking of the snow broke through the silence. Jobey watched her solemn white face, and said nothing. Halfway along the lane she stopped and turned quickly to him.

"Jobey,"

He stopped and looked at her, apprehension drawing down his heavy eyebrows in a worried frown.

"Jobey," Again she got no further. She seemed a long way from him now, more so than ever before. She was near enough for him to put his hands round her waist and lift her out of the snow, to put his lips to the solid smooth coldness of her cheek, but he might as well have tried to kiss the moon. There was a void between them which he didn't know how to bridge, unless she showed him the way.

"Jobey – let's leave it a bit, eh?"

"Leave it?"

"Well, with one thing and another – it's not easy for us, is it?" He held her hand, it was lifeless, but she didn't take it away.

She looked into the distance, "Families – how they do tend to be like lifebelts at times."

His frown deepened.

"You know; they hold you up in trouble, but they surround you. I don't know that I want a lifebelt. I suppose it is nice to have one, but if you're not drowning – well – oh, I don't know, Jobey Rainbow."

Jobey was silent, she would come back to him when she was ready.

She touched the end of his nose. "The best way is for us to meet again after Christmas. That will solve the immediate problem, at any rate."

He could feel her slipping away, or was he just torturing himself? Pop's voice came from afar: 'They're only using you until this thing is over.'

"I'll see you again, Jobey. I've posted you a small present. After Christmas, eh?"

She was away before he could reply, moving quickly and gracefully along the snow-filled lane and leaving him feeling like a discarded snow plough.

He did not move for some time. His face was red-hot and his mind almost numb. He looked towards the house, standing solid and square. Just a house, really, but every brick was something special. The very moon that shone over it was extra special because it shone on them both. Had he been living a dream?

He drove his fist into his hand, shaking his head. He found that tears were streaming down his face, although he had no sensation of weeping.

He knew what his father would say. "The lock-out's over, lad, come down to earth. Come lower than that, come down to Engine Lane where you belong. I told you so. I told you so. I told you so."

Reluctant to turn his back on the house, Jobey stayed on in the lane for another ten minutes. Maybe she would come bouncing out again, like she used to when they went to Misk Hills during the spring and summer. She must, oh dear God, she must.

At that moment the ground began to tremble under his feet. There was a deep rumbling noise which came from everywhere at once, and then it happened. With an almighty thundering roar, he saw the pit-head winding gear disappear. Then a great column of red flame and dust shot hundreds of feet into the air. It went straight up from the pit shaft and sustained itself above it like a giant firework. Jobey stared, horrified. He was witnessing an explosion that was as spectacular as a volcano, but in this case there were men down there in the holocaust.

He wanted to speak to someone. He wanted to be told that what he had just seen hadn't really taken place. It couldn't be. One heard of colliery explosions, but they were just collieries; somewhere or other; this was Moorgreen. His colliery, his people. Now, it had really happened here, right in his own backyard.

A sound of running feet in the snow brought him back to earth. It was Norman Booker, pulling on a coat as he laboured through the snow.

He looked at Jobey with vacant eyes and mouth open.

"She's fired. God Almighty, she's fired."

TEN

And fired she had. At eight-twenty p.m. on Tuesday the twenty-first of December, nineteen hundred and twenty-six. As if Moorgreen had not suffered enough because the pit had not been working, it now began to suffer because it had.

The blower was giving off a continual series of pips which was a call to all rescue teams and ambulance men. People were beginning to arrive at the pit, where the shambles that had been a double-decker cage lay strewn among the wreckage of the winding house. Why the blower was sounding the alarm, Jobey couldn't think. The explosion itself had alerted everybody within a five mile radius.

He could no longer see the stars. A great blanket of sulphurous black and yellow smoke hung over the entire area. There was a fall-out of fine dust which was beginning to coat the snow. It had blown out of the bottom of the pit and to Jobey it smelled of death.

He followed in Norman Booker's footsteps, heading for the pit. He could hear rumbling from under his feet and there was a strange movement on the reservoir. He stopped to watch it for a minute. There was something he could not make out, the water seemed to be slowly moving, but he dismissed it as a trick of the light.

Norman Booker sent messengers to call the local doctors. He was having the offices cleared for use as dressing stations. Desks, files, office furniture were all piled out in the snow to leave the maximum floor space available. The telephone was still working, so he had other pits contacted and asked them to send anything which could be used as an ambulance. Also, he urged, whatever they had in the way of blankets and medical supplies.

All this was very well, but at the moment there was nothing, between the surface and whatever lay below, but a deep naked hole. It gave him vertigo just to think of the way a body would fall into the abyss, and all these people milling around trying to get information. He must get some order out of the chaos.

Lights were fitted up to shine on the top of the shaft, and oil drums and planks laid all round to keep the people back. He called his rescue teams together and explained the situation. The Company owned a mobile winding crane which could lower a skip down the shaft. This was normally held at Mansfield, but as terrible bad luck would have it there had been trouble with the pit cage at Moorgreen's sister colliery at Worksop. The crane had been sent there only the week before, and as it could travel no faster than two miles an hour it would be a two-day job to get it to Moorgreen. The winding machinery itself, which stood back about a hundred and fifty yards, was still intact. The cage had been at the top when the blast struck, so there was plenty of cable on the drum. They must fix some sort of a structure above the shaft, make a cage to get down there, and bring up the wounded or dead. The old cage had weighed ten tons and went up and down the shaft at sixty miles an hour, so they had plenty of safety margin.

Booker drew up a quick plan and a lorry was despatched at once to one of the Company's steel subsidiaries for the necessary girders. His idea was simply for the framework of a steel box to go over the top of the shaft. Pulley wheels could be bolted to the structure and the cables led over these and attached to a make-shift cage. Booker explained to them all that if another blast came up the shaft they would all be fried to a crisp. Not one man gave any sign of hearing the warning, so work began.

Jobey's one idea was to go to the lamp-cabin to watch from its dark interior. He felt like some alien creature of the night. It didn't seem to him that he had one friend in the whole world. He could stand that with Margaret, but without her ... He felt ashamed of himself. At a time when over a hundred men were below ground and helpless, perhaps dead or dying, he was concerned only with his private grief. He tried to put all thoughts of Margaret out of his mind. What could he do to help? When the steel girders arrived he could manhandle them into place. What if they refused his help? At a time like this it would be the ultimate degradation. He had taken all he could for now. No, he would stay in the darkness of the lamp-cabin, watching real people with real grief. He had no part to play, they were not his people any more. He was a thing apart, imprisoned by his conscience. He gravitated to the empty lamp-cabin and its protection. He took the blackness into himself. He was at one with his great anonymous gravelike world, and cocooned in his fortress blanket, he slept.

Rescue teams were despatched to Pinkstone Colliery which joined up with Moorgreen. Dr. Alexander went with them, to see if a road through was possible. It was only an emergency road at best, but it might serve for a rescue attempt. Another team under Seth Sloman, the Under-Manager, went to the Westwood drift in the hope that the roof might have held. Several phones below ground connected to Norman Booker's, and he glanced at the instrument every thirty seconds, willing it to ring. It must ring. What in the name of heaven had happened down there? Could anyone remain alive after such a fearsome explosion as that?

He had a list of everyone below ground, there were a hundred and fifty-seven in all. He drew a plan of where they probably were when the explosion took place. The seam they were working now had been notorious for faults. The roads went up and down like a switchback, gradually rising all the time the further they went away from the shaft. This was important. It may have channelled the blast into the floor or ceiling, and the men at the farthest points would have the best chance of survival. The blast must have started near to the pit bottom, or the explosion would surely not have ripped up to the surface like that; but there was no work being done near the pit bottom. Nobody was working anywhere near the bottom of the shaft, yet that is where the trouble must have begun. He had just got the plans out again, to have a look at where the men should have been, when the office window blasted in, bringing glass all over the desk and his plans. He dropped on the floor, thinking there had been another explosion, cutting his little finger to the bone on a piece of glass.

Nothing happened until the office door was kicked in, and a raging, seething Tony Pandy marched in.

"You can get off the floor, Booker. That was a piece of pit

cage I flung in your window, *you've* not been in any explosion. You let men work on in twice the safety level of gas, but that doesn't matter to you, does it? You knew the barometer readings – *everybody* knew the temperature was going up."

Booker went white. This was just what he had been afraid of. A man like Tony Pandy, a born troublemaker, liking nothing better than to rip down the structure of authority. He would shoot off his mouth to every cheap newspaper in the land.

"What are you blabbing about, you ignorant fool? What sort of talk is this?"

Two or three of the others came running into the office, including an ambulance man, who carefully put the edges of Booker's wound together and bound it up tightly.

"You'll pay for this, you ... This is assault, and damage to Company property."

"If you want to see some damage to Company property, Booker, look out there. Look where the pit-head used to be. And there's more Company property damaged below, a hundred and fifty-odd pieces of it. Down there, where there's not a sound coming from, at the bottom of that bloody great hole. There'll be no white-washing Booker, you've had us all by the throat since the lock-out finished, but the boot's on the other foot now. I've had you marked down, ever since they found old Sam Severn with matches in his pocket after that explosion at Ironbridge. You picked a wrong un that time, Booker ... old Sam Severn never smoked in his life ... *you* had those bloody matches planted on him."

Tony Pandy was beginning to enjoy this, the situation was tailor-made for him.

The door opened again and a lone pole came in with Dobbin at the end of it, "Do you want me Mr. Booker?"

The room took on a deathly silence. This was the very eye of the storm, from where wisdom and courage should emanate, where every word was precious and so was every second. Up to now, all Booker had received was a tirade of abuse and threats from Tony Pandy, and now an offer from Dobbin to go down with his pole!

The Welshman was incensed at the sight of Dobbin.

"You have this half-baked potato." He pointed at Dobbin.

"He ought to be down there with them. He ought to know what's going on. If he was a proper fireman he could stop a shift going on; but he's not ... he's Dobbin, and works for bloody peanuts, and why not? Him being a monkey and all."

"There is a proper fireman, Dobbin is just ..." He stopped himself, what was he doing, arguing with this object?

The Manager suddenly felt the full weight of the job on his shoulders. Year after year he took risks which everyone knew about, but to which, for various reasons, mainly greed, everyone turned a blind eye. Waverley would be here any minute. "What's the trouble Booker? How could this possibly have happened?" Declaring his ignorance, ready to abandon his Manager to the wolves. He was for the chop. Just as he had singled out Joe Bird, now it was his own turn. Well, that was that; but first, he had a job to do.

"Get out!" He turned on Tony Pandy. "If you've nothing to contribute to help your mates, then bloody stop your squealing."

Tony Pandy looked a little shame-faced. "If you need any volunteers, I'm here and ready. But one thing you can bet on, you can put a match to your Manager's certificate."

Norman Booker saw him depart with loathing, then he hurried out to see how the erection of the steel girders was going. The fitters were making a temporary cage and would be ready in about an hour. The telephone rang, and Booker snatched it off its cradle, thinking it might be someone below ground.

"Yes, yes, Booker here."

There was a pause which nearly drove him mad.

"Who's there. Who is it?"

Then a voice said "Sloman here, Norman, at Westwood. The drift seems solid. The roof's down all the way, what shall we do?"

"Get them digging, man. Try to break through, but if you do break through, test for air current at once. If there's anything at all, put stoppings up at once. Mustn't get a through draught, in case there's fire; now get off the line."

"Yes sir."

Booker slammed the receiver down. "Damn and blast, Westwood's had it. Let's hope for better luck at Pinkstone.

One of you men, go and get Sloman back here. Don't want him wasting his time with a shovel."

"Some men here from the press, sir. What shall I tell them?"

Sid Shaw, one of the overmen, looked distinctly uncomfortable as several reporters started to crowd the Manager.

"Tell them we don't know a bloody thing yet," The press men recognised him as being in authority, and tried a few questions.

"How many men down there?"

"Are you in touch? ... Have you had any word from them?"

Booker held up a hand. "Gentlemen, I'm sure you don't wish to hamper the rescue work. Now my Under-Manager, Mr. Sloman, will be back in a few minutes, I'll get him to answer your questions – as far as we are able. We have had no contact yet. All I can say right now is that a hundred and fifty-seven men are trapped down below. Please leave me alone now."

The reporters disappeared, picking up personal stories, looking for men who, for some small reason, had not turned up for work. Looking for a large family with the father down below. They had their own jobs to do.

Joe Bird appeared on the scene, talking to the men, and weighing up the chances. They rallied round him, as in the old days, but there was to be no speech this time. The Manager saw him, but said nothing. A few hours earlier he would have had him run off the place for trespassing.

The telephone went again, it was Dr. Alexander. "We're not making much headway at this Pinkstone end, Norman, every road is collapsed in. Don't know where the hell I am here. Can you find Jobey Rainbow? He's the only one who might know where to start. Unless I miss my guess, we've got to work from this end. How are you going with the cage?"

"Won't be too long now if it all works. We'll have to get it ready though, and Lord knows what we'll be lowering into. I'll get off the phone now, keep trying. I'll have somebody find Jobey Rainbow."

Norman Booker went back to the steel erectors. They were still drilling and bolting, but at last the primitive cage was ready. It was clad with wire mesh and would hold about ten men with their equipment.

A large crowd had gathered now, which parted for a moment to let the Waverley Brothers up to the front. One or two boos went up from the crowd, but nobody took much notice. John Waverley took Booker aside.

"This is a bad business Norman, a bad business. Any idea what happened yet?"

Booker looked very thoughtful. "Bound to be gas, Mr. Waverley, but what triggered it off? Been very fiery just lately, the whole pit has. We've been working on with readings of up to three percent. What with the break for Christmas coming and ..."

"Three percent! You'll get us all bloody shot. What are you going to tell the Inspectors? Have we any canaries left?"

"Balls to the canaries ... and ..." Booker pulled himself up just in time.

"You've had my reports, Mr. Waverley. I'm not trying to put the onus on to anybody else, it was my decision, but you had my reports." He spoke wearily as if wanting to be done with the subject.

"Has the Inspector shown up yet? He's going to take some handling." Waverley glanced round apprehensively.

"No, he's not here yet, but he's been notified. There's one of the men already told me he's going to make all the trouble he can. I'm finished anyway, a court of inquiry will tear me to pieces." He ran a hand through his hair and looked at John Waverley, who had aged ten years in as many minutes. "Never mind about me, let's see who we can save from that mess below ground."

The telephone rang again. John Waverley looked sharply at Booker, and snatched the ear piece off the cradle. Just as quickly, the Manager snatched it from Waverley, with a withering look. "Yes. Yes."

"Alexander here again."

"Oh, it's you."

"Yes. Now listen, Norman, I've been thinking. Who's going down when the cage is ready? Who'll be in charge?"

"Seth Sloman. Why?" He had already forgotten about the press men.

"I thought so. There's bound to be dust down there as thick as a pudding. It only wants triggering. He thinks I'm stressing the danger too much. Dust once caused a series of explosions which spread through five pits and killed over a thousand people. That dust is so fine it'll go off like an ammunition dump."

"It's had plenty of stone dust on it."

"It's had plenty of sand on it as well, putting out gob-fires. There's no dust on earth worse than sand. That may be part of the trouble we've had already."

"All right, I'll tell him to watch it."

The Doctor would not be put off. "Dust that's been settled for years will be floating around ready to ..."

"Yes. Yes, don't keep on about it, I'll tell him. Have you got a way through yet? Surely things can't be as bad as all that. You're five miles from our pit shaft, where you are now."

"It's bad Norman. The explosions must have come along the main gate like bombs dropping. I've heard of it happening before. You get a fireball travelling along and all hell breaks loose as it passes by. There's about six different roads here and only one leads through to Moorgreen. I don't know 'tother from which' at the moment. We're digging the lot until you can find Jobey Rainbow. Better send some more men if you've got any to spare."

"Right. Let me know when you've sorted it out."

There was no shortage of volunteers to strengthen the digging party at Pinkstone. Extra men were also sent off with orders not to come back without Jobey Rainbow. Meanwhile, almost under their noses, Jobey had curled up in his cabin and was now asleep.

The temporary winding house was ready at last, and Seth Sloman went aboard with nine other picked men from the pit's own rescue squad. They were all hard, fit men and rigorously trained for just such an emergency. They piled on first their picks, axes, shovels, ropes, telephone with cable on drum, oxygen, face masks, everything the rescuers might need, and then they all sat on top. Seth Sloman looked a little white as they prepared to lower away. Tater Varley settled along-side him, easing himself comfortably on to an oxygen cylinder. A system of signalling was laid on from the top of the shaft to the winding house, and all was ready.

"Keep paying out the cable," Norman Booker shouted them their last instructions. "We'll lower you about one foot a second for the first five hundred and fifty feet, then the last fifty feet a lot slower, but keep us in touch all the time. If there's any trouble and the line goes dead, we'll bring you up right away."

The silent faces all nodded at him, then they had disappeared down the shaft. A great silence settled over the area now they were gone. It was five-thirty in the morning, but all the relatives who had been there all night came out from the various offices where they had been talking, drinking tea and cat-napping. Everyone spoke in whispers and all eyes were on the Manager, who had the telephone to his ear. The press men stood as closely to him as they dare, and although he eyed them with some suspicion, he raised no objection. He looked towards the first-aid room where three doctors were asleep on stretchers. No sense in them losing sleep, they would be needed when the cage returned.

* * *

There was a strange undefinable smell as the ten men watched the walls of the shaft go by. They had breathing masks in place but not actually in use. They were hot cumbersome things and the men all hoped there would be no need to use them. Seth Sloman had the telephone to his ear. They had 'clannie' lamps for testing for gas, and six canaries in separate cages.

"What's happening?" Booker asked.

"We're going down that's all." Sloman's voice was a trifle unsteady.

"Keep talking", Booker spoke again. "Doesn't matter what you say. Sing, if you can't think of anything else."

The press men came in a little closer. "What are they saying Mr. Booker?" "What are they saying?"

Booker held up his hand. "Just keeping in touch, that's all."

Seth Sloman spoke again, "Damned funny smell."

"Is it gas? What's it like?"

"Not gas. Can't place it. How far to go now?"

"You're about half way. Is the cage swinging?"

"It is a bit, and spinning. Hope it doesn't hit anything. We'll go arse over tip if anything's sticking out. You keep quiet now and I'll do the talking. I think you'd better slow us up a bit. We've got quite a lot of movement on now."

They felt the slowing down almost at once. The signalling system was obviously working.

"That's better. We've got the breathing masks on now. Hope we don't have to keep them like this." Sloman went on talking for another few minutes, then Booker broke in.

"You've only about fifty feet to go. Guide us from your end when you can see the stop."

Sloman held out his lamp and saw the brickwork come into view. "Steady now, nearly there." The cage almost stopped, then trickled on another few feet. "Hold it there! We've arrived."

"What can you see? Is anybody there?" Booker's voice came quickly now.

"Give us a chance. Can't see anybody. Everything's as quiet as the gr..." He checked himself in the middle of the word.

They shone their lamps around, "Nobody got to the bottom of the shaft, that's for certain." Tater Varley voiced their thoughts, "I don't like it. Where are they all? Surely somebody should be here out of a hundred and fifty-seven?"

Sloman looked at him, "For God's sake shut it, Varley. It's bad enough without your opinions."

"What's that? I can't hear you." Booker demanded down the phone. Sloman rolled up his eyes in exasperation. "We can't see a thing yet. Plenty of dust still in the air. I'm testing for gas now ... Hmm, not bad. Hardly any gas here at all, thank God. It's masks off for a minute. Tater, bring a canary, leave the rest here, and Tater, if that canary blinks one eye, I want to know."

"Something here!" A voice came from the darkness about ten feet away. It was Charlie Wildgoose; he had volunteered when he saw Tater in the rescue party. Tater felt pleased about that; it was a first step towards healing the wounds.

"We've found a body I think," Sloman spoke into the phone. Booker did not answer. He was asking himself what he had expected. They must find another and another and another, perhaps one-hundred-and-fifty-seven in all. They had a pit full of bodies, and he had killed them all. The cold morning air fanned his hot cheeks as his brain went numb and refused to acknowledge his ears. He stared straight ahead in a hot flood of incomprehension.

"Can't make it out," said Charlie. "Surely it's not a man." He touched the thing on the floor with his foot. It rustled like a bunch of burnt newspapers.

"Don't do that." Seth Sloman came up. It was a gruesome thing to find in the quiet blackness. It strung up their taut nerves to breaking point, but they had to press on.

"Two bodies," Sloman spoke into the phone. "They can't be separated or recognised. Don't let anybody near them. I'm putting them in the cage. I'm going to have a look along the main gate now. Be back in a few minutes to report."

"Seth! Seth! Leave a man on the phone."

"Of course. Now leave us alone to get on with it."

They left Charlie Wildgoose with his grisly find, which he loaded on to the cage and sat beside, with the telephone on his knee.

Sloman led them away, quietly. Charlie could just hear Sloman's voice in a loud whisper.

"Tater, come in front with that bird."

Then everything was quiet as Charlie sat in the cage with just a small pool of light, which showed up something he was trying not to look at. He had never been a man of great imagination, but his eyes kept turning themselves in the direction of what Sloman had described as two men. He found his head was turned away from it but his eyes were screwing round painfully, trying to see – as if his eyes had a separate existence.

He decided he was not scared. He would turn his head and look at the mummified remains. It was just that it was so quiet, and he was so tensed up and half expecting another explosion. He imagined himself being ejected up the shaft like a shell from a gun, possibly in enforced proximity with the other occupants of the cage. He wished the others would come back. He was not frightened – not Charlie Wildgoose. To prove it, he would turn his head and look at the burnt thing – in a short while. Not right now; there was no screaming hurry.

He didn't have to prove anything.

He sat for another minute until he heard voices again. He couldn't recognise Sloman. It was funny that someone else should be doing so much talking. Suddenly he realised they had found somebody. In fact, he could now make out the sound of many boots. They were coming back with a large party of survivors!

He brought the telephone into action without waiting to hear any more. Booker shouted in reply, a trifle hysterically:

"Yes, Yes, who's that?"

"Charlie Wildgoose. Mr. Sloman has found some men."

"Alive? You mean alive?"

"Yes. Don't know how many – sounds like a lot."

Booker's voice broke for the first and last time. Then Charlie heard him speaking to someone at the top. He could hear cheering in the background. What an agony of mind for those who had been waiting all night. Then they were all round him. Sloman took the incinerated bodies off the make-shift cage and had it loaded with survivors.

"Injured men first," he called. "Tater, you go up with them and come back with the cage. If it swings too badly, slow it down – Now, go man, go."

He watched carefully, sorting out the dead they had brought with them, and putting them aside. Some of the men had brought parts of bodies and these, too, were laid reverently alongside the dead.

He spoke into a fixed telephone near the bottom of the shaft, "Norman?"

"Yes Seth."

"Be as quick as you can. I don't know how much time we've got."

"Why?" What's the trouble? What can we do?"

"Nothing, except hurry. Gas is swirling around in pockets." He looked at the dead canary which Tater had passed to him without a word.

"Seth, I've got another team standing by."

"Not likely. Send the cage back empty, except for Varley to steady it."

Booker asked the question he had been plucking up the courage to ask, "Seth?"

"Norman?"

"Seth, how many? How many men have you got there?"

"There's about sixty, including injured. Some are not going to live. Then there's some dead."

"How many? How many dead?"

"You'll have to sort it out up there, Norman. I'll send everything up. It'll be a messy job."

Booker did not answer at first then said, more to himself, "I'll have a room got ready, get the windows blacked out somehow."

"Be quick with the unloading, Norman. I'm going to have a look in 67 district."

Booker took a breath to tell Sloman to be careful, then closed his mouth again. The cage was at the top.

Sloman put another bird in the small cage, passed it to Charlie Wildgoose and took two more men, heading now in the opposite direction to where they had been.

They passed along the main gate, walking strung out in single file for safety, only to witness even worse sights. The frightful force of the explosion had caught a ganger and his pony just coming out of the stable. Although rescue teams were trained for their job, they now felt distinctly chilled in the stomach. In the next hundred yards they found seven more bodies all bearing the same horrific burns, none of them was recognisable. Charlie trod on a pony's hoof and fell on his back, swearing. It came into his mind that he had seen a pony's hoof made into an inkwell somewhere.

Very near to the bottom of the shaft was an old working which no-one had travelled for several years. Not even Jobey and Dr. Alexander had been along here. The entrance had been closed off by a big iron door which was now missing, but the whole entrance surround had been blown outwards into the main gate. Surely the explosion could not have originated from here, but it looked a lot like it. Booker said the explosion had been very near to the pit bottom, and he was usually right.

Sloman spoke more to himself than to anyone else. "I suspect air must have been leaking into these old workings, place could have been full of gas. This coal was soft as putty, just the right texture for spontaneous combustion. Like leaving a time bomb. Sam Watson said, a while back, there was a gob-stink from in here, and he's got a nose like a ferret. He said these old workings were 'breathing' and nobody believed him."

He stopped his men and they had a good look round. Sure enough, the great iron door was found mangled up like a piece of tinsel paper. It had blown into the main gate and almost fetched the roof down with the force of the impact. He wondered if a fall of stone had released a pocket of gas. But what would have triggered it off?

He entered the old workings, testing for gas. He kept his lamp held high in front of him, watching the flame all the time for the tell-tale rise, which indicated firedamp. The man behind him kept his lamp low, watching for black-damp. Sloman's flame started to rise almost at once.

"Masks on!" he shouted urgently. There was gas here all right, far too much of it. There was a lot of dust about, too. The darkness seemed so solid, it would not part to allow the rays of the lamp through. Sloman had a creepy sensation. The place smelled of death. There was an evil atmosphere about it, or did he just imagine that because this was where the explosion appeared to have started? He peered into the old blackness and shuddered his skin into goose-pimples.

"There be Dragons!" he muttered, feeling a horror he could not explain. The canary was dead.

"Let's get out of here," Sloman said into his mask. He signalled to the others.

The party carried on. Bodies were found at intervals, but long before the coal face was reached the road was closed in by falls of stone. They rapped on the metal lines which carried the trucks, in the hope that there might be some reply. Keeping quiet and hoping, praying, they held their breath in the great blackness.

"There's nobody there," one of them whispered.

"Quiet," hissed Sloman. They held their breath again. Listening. Willing a reply to come from behind the stone and coal.

After several more attempts, they gave it up and decided to return with the news.

"Must be at least fifty men in that district," Sloman told

them. "Hope Tater has got the others all up." They started back, and hesitated once again at the entrance to the old workings. The place held Sloman like a snake holds a rabbit. It had not yet finished its diabolical work. Sloman took them in once again, just as if some loathsome disciple of the devil was beckoning them into the unspeakable cave where they had now kept their appointment with death.

It would be very satisfying to solve the mystery, and Sloman was sure that this was its source. He adjusted the lamp and again took readings for gas, but he had been too slow this time. His cry of 'Masks on' was very faint, and he turned to see the men bunched behind him, instead of being strung out as they should have been. The tension and horror of what they had been through had relaxed everybody's vigilance, and Sloman knew he was going under. Only Charlie Wildgoose was hanging back. Sloman swung his lamp to try to warn him. The glass came into contact with a piece of sharp metal, exposing the naked flame.

ELEVEN

Meanwhile, Tater had sent all the survivors to the top, then stayed behind to do his own investigating. He headed for 49 district with all possible speed. He stopped for nothing, ignoring bodies of men and ponies and unspeakable bundles. He could not believe that all these good men had perished. Sam Watson, Matty Wilson, The Bulldog, Bert Honey, Pokey Jordan, Sid Perkins, Philip Burgin, Alf Wharmby and a host of others. They were not all dead, it was past comprehension. He was not so much bothered about Pokey Jordan. It was *his* bad luck to have been transferred to Moorgreen only a week ago.

He had seen their coats in the locker room before he came down. They looked normal and reassuring, as if the men must reappear at any moment and put them on. The men were as near as stretching out a hand for their coats. Why would the coats be all hanging in rows like that if their owners were not coming to fetch them?

He came at last to a phone, fastened to a bracket on the wall. So far, he had needed all his breath and energy to get through the minor falls of roof and broken trucks which lay at all crazy angles. Tater lifted the phone and cranked the handle, thinking he would get through to the pit top. He leaned over the fixture, his gaunt face sucking in air, when he heard a voice through the phone:

"Thank God. Who are you? We are trapped by water."

Tater almost dropped the phone. He had made contact with more survivors. "Who is it? Who's speaking?"

"This is Philip Burgin. There are forty of us here. The water came up behind us. It's lying in the switchback section, forcing us forward. I've got to leave this phone in a minute, so listen. The water must be still coming in. As soon as there's enough of it, it'll come down at you and fill up the road right down as far as the pit bottom. I don't know how long that will be but it's bound to come up here after that, and drown us all like rats. We're digging towards the old thin seam. If we can get into that we'll maybe get into the Pinkstone workings. It's our only chance. Tell Norman Booker to come and find us from the Pinkstone end. Tell him to find the route on the plans. He must get Jobey Rainbow on the job, he knows these old workings better than any of us. Don't forget anything. Get back now and report. You can't do anything from there. Who are you?"

"This is Tater Varley."

"Good old Tater. Get going now. Have got to put the phone down. Up to my knees in water. Tell Booker everything. Get Jobey."

The phone went dead and Tater stared hard at the earpiece. Forty of them trapped by water in the switchback section.

He ran back to the bottom of the shaft. The cage was standing there, empty.

Tater snatched the phone, "That you, Mr. Booker?"

"No. He's sorting out the bodies into boxes, do you want him?"

"Yes. This is Tater Varley. Tell him I've found some survivors. Put him on as quick as you can."

About thirty seconds elapsed, then a breathless Norman Booker answered.

"Yes, Tater. How many?"

"Forty, Mr. Booker, they're trapped up at the face in 49 district. The switchback section's full of water and it's still coming in, it's bound to reach here soon. They're trying to break through the old thin seam. If they can do that they might be able to get into the Pinkstone workings and out that way."

"Water? Water? What water are you talking about? There's no water in that district."

"There is now. It's coming in from somewhere right enough. Now listen. Philip Burgin spoke to me on the telephone, I don't know who's with him but he said there's about forty of them. Burgin said to get Jobey. He says they've no chance except to get out at the Pinkstone end."

"Have you seen the water?"

"No. I just picked up the phone and there they were. Came straight back to warn you; and to fetch Mr. Sloman. The water may come down with a rush when it starts."

"Right, Varley. Well done. Get the others and ..."

He got no further. The whole of the ground around the pit-head shook visibly as a terrible explosion took place below ground.

Tater felt the pit 'suck' ... the dreaded sudden lowering of the air pressure which preceded an explosion. It was no use trying to run, he was for it now. He couldn't make a noise, he was speechless with horror.

It was on the opposite side of the shaft to Tater, and the brickwork took a lot of the shock into itself, but a fireball screamed along the main gate, where Seth Sloman and his fellow rescuers had just blown themselves into very small fragments.

Tater heard it coming, and fell onto his knees. He tried to claw himself into the ground as the fireball approached, screaming like a demented soul as it played a high pressure tune on the surrounding air. It created awful vacuums and just as quickly filled them in with white heat, leaving a roaring tunnel of fire in its tortured wake.

Tater grasped one of his hands with the other, in his lonely agony it was some small comfort. In a few seconds it was over. Tater could hardly see at all, but he could smell burning flesh. Surely not his own, he could not feel any pain. His chest felt as if a giant hand had reached into his lungs and pulled them inside-out. The dust was choking him. He ran a hand through his hair and found he was bald, every small whisker burned away. His back and shoulders felt tight and unnatural. He felt along with his fingers and they sank into the soft spongy flesh as if it were a pudding. He pressed again and his fingers sank in once more. Oh God, what had happened to him?

He felt for the iron rail which would lead him to the pit bottom and the life-giving cage. If it was there and still working, he might be able to get back to the surface. He found the rail and crawled along beside it, painfully slowly, feeling every inch of the way so that he should not fall into the sump. He need not have bothered. He was so shocked and disorientated that he was travelling away from the cage, not towards it. Every stiff grotesque movement of arms and legs carried him away from the shaft, towards the cold black menacing water, waiting like a great beast to envelop him in its pain-killing arms. Then, as if it could wait no longer it came down from the slope towards him, cooling his body as it flowed around his naked form.

Tater knew then what had happened, he knew he had been crawling the wrong way, but he was not beaten yet. He felt a wooden door floating by and placed an almost useless arm over it, and hung on. He might yet get washed down to the shaft and the cage, with its half chance of life, if it still worked.

It was a great pity that, in the face of such resilience and tenacity, the fates did not look more kindly upon Tater; but the next explosion was to release Tater from his poor useless body.

Tater had always said he wanted to die with his lamp full. When bodies had been found in previous explosions where men had been trapped, it was usually possible to tell by the amount of oil left in their lamps, how long the men had lived before the air ran out. Empty lamps meant death had been slow and lingering ... possibly even by starvation. Tater had lived hard and died hard.

Norman Booker fell onto one knee and was violently sick. Nobody paid any attention to him. They were all stunned, as the ground heaved and cracked. With a noise like an express train the earth shuffled its strata about and settled back into place. Booker looked at the dead telephone in his hand, and then at John Waverley, who stared back open-mouthed. They each knew what the other was thinking.

The Manager stayed on his knees. The suspense, the shock, the responsibility, the coming public degradation, were just pressing his head into the ground. The blackened snow seemed unreal to him. For a small minute his mind rejected the awful reality and tried to hide from its duty. In a delirium of warm self-comfort he floated away from his body and looked down on the pathetic creature that he was. He saw a frail human form. He saw the herd instinct of the crowd, which would rogue him out as some brutal primeval force had ordained. He saw the whole childlike frailty of mankind, with great clarity. He stiffened his shoulders and lifted his head.

Was he intended to run with this herd, or was he not the Manager to whom they all looked for advice? He was going to get those forty men out through the Pinkstone workings if he had to dig them out with his bare hands. It was eight a.m. on Wednesday, twenty-second of December, they must have enough air for at least a day or two. God willing, he would have a Christmas box for forty families at least.

The water which had trapped them would, in all probability, have protected them from the later explosions and the fire. But if water was still going in from the reservoir, or somewhere, there was no telling how long they had to live. They could drown, or just use up the air they had. And where – oh where on earth was Jobey Rainbow?

He rang for Dr. Alexander and gave him the news about the trapped men. "Get here as soon as you can, Gordon, we've got to go through the plans. It's that end or nothing, now. How are you getting along?"

"We're in about half a mile. Clearing falls about every hundred yards. I feel whacked, how are you?"

Booker took a deep breath. "I've had my moments, but I'm all right now. I'm beginning to think bloody Rainbow's run away. He must have heard the explosion and gone to ground somewhere. No other explanation. The police have been everywhere. You pay a man extra for all these bloody years for being on call for rescue, and then the first time you want him the bugger's missing."

"Have you tried your house?"

"My house, what do you mean?"

"You know damned well what I mean. One thing I can tell you for sure, wherever else he is, he's not run away."

A murmur went up from the crowd, and Booker looked up to see the cause. Jobey was walking forward briskly to see what was happening. Hands in his pockets, the great powerful legs thrusting forward; even in inaction he looked a powerhouse of strength and energy.

"Well, sod me!" The Manager nearly dropped the phone.

"What's the matter? What's happened? What is it, Norman?"

"It's Jobey Rainbow, large as bloody life."

"Thank God for that. I'm coming right over."

TWELVE

The pressmen were taking photographs of Jobey. The way the crowd opened up to let him through told them that this was the Jobey Rainbow they had been hearing about. The man who had the first-hand knowledge of all the old workings, who had the temperament, and certainly the strength, to put some faith back into the hearts of the still-waiting families.

"Get them out, Jobey."

"Bless you, Jobey – get 'em lad."

The cries swelled into a cheer, and as if by magic the months of bitterness fell away from them all. In the greater crisis that now faced them they would have clutched at straws – but this was no straw. This was the man who had protected the pit and the drift at Westwood, almost single-handed. Their desperation now gave Jobey superhuman powers.

The wave of sudden approval carried him forward to the Manager's Office where Booker was waiting – a little apprehensively. So short a time ago he had deliberately engineered Jobey's dismissal, connived with his wife to stop Margaret seeing him again, had delighted in the thought of being rid of the big untutored, socially unacceptable Jobey Rainbow; and here was that same Jobey, striding in, genuinely pleased to see him.

He held out a hand. "Lot of men trapped in 49 section, Jobey, there's very little time, are you with us?"

"I am that, Mr. Booker, I am un all." He shook the Manager's hand as if nothing had happened. "What do you want me to do?"

More pressmen were arriving all the time as the news spread like wildfire. A lot of the crowd now set off for Pinkstone Colliery, as it became obvious that the Moorgreen shaft was finished. Relations who had been up all night set off to walk the five miles in the snow. There was a chance that their man would be amongst the ones still alive.

The Manager had a meeting of overmen, Mine Inspectors and Federation Officials. The plans were rapidly considered and it was soon obvious that the trapped men were only about thirty feet from the thin seam, but they would have to leave their present line of advance and strike downwards at a slight angle. This would take them away from the coal and into the shale and rock strata where the going was tough. "No explosives, so they'll have to knock it all off with the point of the pick. How long is that going to take?" Norman Booker posed the question.

Various estimates were given, anything from one to three days was suggested. Dr. Alexander was doing some calculations himself, he wouldn't trust anybody else.

"We don't know how long the air is going to last them – we don't know how far the water is in behind them, but it just might be as little as two or three days, and then there's the water itself. It may not be just a question of air, we ought to assume we've only got a couple of days. Now if we can get to the thin seam and arrive at the point where they're digging, we can meet them part way. Should be plenty of time then. We can put them some air in from our end. The question I should like answered is, how fast is the water going in? If your theory's right, Norman, and it's going down from the reservoir ..." he stopped speaking. No-one volunteered an opinion. "Now bring Jobey in, I want him to see the plans."

The Manager was aware that the Doctor was taking the job of rescue on to himself at the moment, but he was too tired to object. He must have a couple of hours' sleep, then he would be ready again. But there was a niggling in his mind. Something was wrong with the Doctor's theory, which he could not fathom out just now.

Jobey came in, looked the plans over, and saw it immediately.

"Last year we broke through from the switchback into the thin seam, I know it clearly. You know what that means?"

They all nodded. The words sounding like a death knell, Jobey continued, "The thin seam must be already flooded. They are tunnelling straight towards the water. The moment they get near enough it will burst through and they're as good as dead." No-one spoke. The room was deathly quiet as each man repeated the words to himself. Jobey spoke again. He turned his back on the plans, which he never trusted anyway. "There's one way we can do it."

They all looked at him now. The Manager almost screamed at Jobey's ponderous method of delivering an announcement. He clenched his fists, longing to shout "Get on with it."

"Remember Billy Musson's Colliery?" This was a very small concern which John Waverley had bought out and then terminated. "Mr. Waverley had them stopped because we were just below their seam and we couldn't keep the roof up. That seam was being taken out of solid rock. They must be just below it, and the water won't be in there. There's a chance we can cut a chimney down to them from there."

Booker slapped the table. "By God he's right. *If* we can get to them before they reach the water, we'll have them out yet."

Dr. Alexander was already digging out maps and making calculations. He took a bundle of them under his arm and they set off for Billy Musson's pit, which had not been worked for two years.

Fitters were rushed there to get the fan going to ventilate the workings. Jobey and Dr. Alexander went down at the head of another rescue squad. The Manager stayed at the top of the shaft with the telephone off the hook and listening hard.

* * *

Down in 49 district Philip Burgin kept them tunnelling. The air was already heavy, and the men doing the work were changed every ten minutes. They slept as well as they could in the dusty atmosphere, trying to find a spot to accommodate their hip bones. There were several deputies present, but Philip Burgin was in command. He allowed no lamps to be lit except the ones in use for the diggers. It was not the oil he wanted to save, but the air. He had made a few calculations and then given up. He didn't know how long the air would last, then – he wasn't sure that he wanted to know. They worked desperately, but were not very hopeful of rescue, unless it came from outside.

The Bulldog decided to call on his own rescue service. From

the blackness he raised his best preaching voice in supplication:

"Oh God, who has ordained all things in heaven and earth, and underneath the earth; look kindly upon these Thy children in their desperate need. Grant unto them, oh Lord, that they may live to glorify Thy name. Deliver us from this awful place, oh God, and we shall be Thy servants for the rest of our days; Thy most humble and grateful servants. We will speak Thy name and tell of the miracle Thou hast wrought for the benefit of these Thy wretched unworthy children. We shall glorify Thy name over all the earth." His voice was raised now and they all knew his arms would be raised also, although he could not be seen.

"Pray with me brothers to the all-hallowed Mighty Father." A general silence fell on the men, and the diggers paused for a second. Philip Burgin's voice cut through the dark like a whiplash, "Keep digging men! I'm giving the orders here."

There was a general hush as the mens' material selves came into conflict with their desire to shelter inside their religion. Philip Burgin represented their physical immediate need to keep digging, the practical approach which said 'Here is your way out'. He was common sense. He was a man who wasted neither words nor energy. He was in charge because they recognised his efficiency. He was a very positive character, had got his head above the crowd on merit. He had their respect.

But a call much older and stronger than Burgin's efficiency was stirring within them. The great parent God, whose omnipotence might just possibly work the miracle, was right there among them. Consciously or unconsciously the Bulldog was calling help for them from across the ages. With his trousers up at half mast and his turned-up boots, he was at once a foolish caricature and yet a sophisticated powerhouse. And so the picks stopped, and heads were bared, and the Bulldog was King. Burgin fumed. While the Bulldog was making his ridiculous bargains and squirming at the feet of his God, they were wasting precious time and air. But spend it they did.

The Bulldog spoke again: "Our Father which art in Heaven

. . ." And not a sound was heard except the unison of voices. Soaring away, taking away with them a little of the fear and the anxiety. Leaving in its place a little of the magic potion that quietens hearts; distilled from ingredients so secret that even the Bulldog did not know the formula.

But the Bulldog was still human. Sensing his victory over Burgin he carried on to spoil it all with a theory of his own.

"This is what comes of disturbing the graves of long dead trees. The gases are the dead trees' defensive weapons. They are spirits creeping out of the coal and taking revenge."

"He's stark bloody staring. Sit down, you daft bugger."

Pokey Jordan brought the service to an abrupt close.

There was a last small silence before work started again but in that few seconds Pokey heard a strange sound. He thought he recognised the noise, and set off with a lamp to investigate. Men were stretched out flat on the ground, resting, so as to use as little air as possible. He turned off the main gate into a cross gate and there sure enough was a pony. Alf Wharmby stood with it stroking its neck. He had just been giving it a pinch of snuff. It curled its top lip as if about to sneeze and then nudged Alf as if for another pinch. Pokey knocked Alf's round figure flying and caught hold of the pony's bridle.

"What the hell are you playing at, Wharmby? You think more of this bloody pony than you do of your wife. You think more of this bloody pony than you do of all of us, you great twat." He pulled the animal along the main gate to where most of the men were resting.

"Look what bloody Wharmby was hiding back there. His blasted pony. Sucking in great dollops of air with its great hairy belly. Somebody sit on its neck because I'm going to put a pick through its head before it uses any more."

"No you're not." Alf Wharmby knew he was pushing his luck, but he thought the world of 'Sweetie'. The pony was small and fat and had a lot in common with Alf.

Sid Perkins pressed forward. He was lodging at Pokey's house again, now that he was earning. Pokey was a man who had his own priorities, his philosophy being, 'a slice off a cut loaf's never missed'.

"Hold the bugger, Sid" Pokey charged the pony from the side and it went down immediately. Sid Perkins sat on its neck so it could not move. Alf Wharmby threw himself on the pony's head.

"No you don't!" he shouted. "You'll have to put that pick through me first."

"Then take the bugger through your ribs," shouted Pokey, and swung the pick downwards. Alf twisted to one side like lightning, the pick just shaving his roll of fat. It entered Sweetie's head at a bad angle and didn't get the brain at all. Taking a more deliberate aim, Pokey put in a second blow which was on target, and the animal wasted no more precious air.

"I'll have a slice off his bloody ribs if we're not out of here by tomorrow," Pokey grunted.

"I'm covered in blood. Place's like a slaughter-house." Sid Perkins set off to have a wash in the black dusty water which was rising behind them all the time.

Burgin went along to see Sam Watson. He had been near to the explosion and was terribly burnt. They had carried Sam with them. Pieces of burnt flesh kept coming away from him. He seemed mercifully unconscious just now. Matty Wilson was sitting alongside him, as Burgin put the lamp down to look at the sorry sight that had once been one of the best colliers in the pit.

Matty cradled the injured man's head in his lap and spoke softly to him so no-one else could hear: "Hang on Sam, we'll be out of here before too long." There were no thoughts now of money in the bank, the men had been good friends once ... at school and for a while afterwards, playing football, courting, laughing and being young. Eventually their characters had hardened into their different moulds, shaped and case-hardened by the dread necessity of constantly pitting their manhood against the coal.

"We'll take the dogs on Misk Hills again Sam ... your Sandy and my Rex. Smell the green wind coming off the mowing grass. That's what we're missing down here Sam, a friendly wind pushing the birds up'ards and filling your lungs that full ... it's like you've just had a fag. And it's had to serve for a fag many a time, eh? Only don't go Sam, don't go."

There was an unnatural stillness in Sam's body ... to be that still or to be dead ... there was no difference. He let out a noise like a crow.

The skin was bright red and all puckered up in places. In others the lymphatic fluid poured from enormous blisters which broke to reveal the white bone underneath. Burgin looked at Matty Wilson, who shook his head. If two-thirds of the body skin is burnt, then death follows quickly, he had read somewhere. He picked up the lamp and shone it on Sam's face. He looked already dead. Matty said, "This one's not going to do any digging, but that makes no odds ..."

Burgin stiffened at the words, "Look Matty, we're getting out of here, understand? And it won't be your mate's prayers that do it either. It'll be men with picks and shovels, and I'm going to see they have enough air to do it."

"Jobey'll find us. Him and the Doctor'll know where we are. You spoke to Tater on the phone didn't you?"

"How do we know that Tater passed on the message? He may not have had time to get back. You heard the other explosions, like the rest of us."

Nothing more was said. Sam Watson died quite peacefully, while some of the men grunted and sweated, and some tried without much success to get to sleep. Alf Wharmby sat alongside Sweetie, patting the still warm body and feeding his hate till it rose in his gorge in a great lump of impotent fury.

Unknowingly they were making good headway towards the sudden death which waited silently for them at the end of the tunnel. They began to wonder if they were going to get away with it, and Philip Burgin urged them on.

"Even if we can't get through the Pinkstone workings, at least it'll give us some air when we break through. There may be falls all over the place but we'll get some air."

Matty Wilson voiced a fear which had remained unspoken until now.

"With all those explosions, it's possible that we're in the only bit that remains standing. What happens then? The lamps are already going dim, that's oxygen shortage. When the lamps go out we shall have about twelve hours to live. Twelve hours of panting and sucking and convulsions in this bloody great hole."

"Christ, Matty, shut up", Burgin shouted at him. "If you don't like it I'll sit on your neck while Pokey puts his pick in.

That'll save you from sucking and panting. Save us from your self-pity as well. Don't you think we all know that we need oxygen?"

Matty scowled at him, "Now I'll give you something to think about. What if Tater Varley wasn't part of a rescue party? What if he was trapped there just like the rest of us? Did he actually say he was part of a rescue party? No, he didn't because you didn't give him a chance. He could be swirling about now in that water back there and *nobody* knows we're alive. Don't give us false hopes, Burgin. We're all in this together. I say it's time for cards on the table and let's see where we stand."

There was general approval for Matty's suggestion, so work stopped for a while. Philip Burgin started the ball rolling:

"We'll have no light to work by soon. What's more, the air won't oxygenate our muscles any more, so we'll just have to lie down and die. But, before that happens, I'll give us about eighteen hours from when the lamps go out, so, the point I'm making is, don't let's talk ourselves into an early grave."

"We're already in the bloody grave." Pokey spat into the darkness. Whenever he made a statement he always emphasized it with a gob from the seemingly inexhaustible supply in his lungs. "We're all bleedin' buried all right. The spirits have got us, the bloody lot of us. If you don't believe me ask 'Creeping Jesus' there. He's all right, he's had one foot in heaven for years. Got some good friends up there, has the Bulldog. Heard a story once about a Bulldog that shit in the gateway to heaven ..."

There was a resounding noise of shovel on bone, which echoed round the group like a gong. Pokey shot forward, and took no further interest in the proceedings. The Bulldog had got him with a full blooded swipe with the back of a shovel. He took full credit for it. "The Lord works in a mysterious way sometimes. Even a common shovel can be an instrument in His hands." It was no use having one foot in heaven if you couldn't speak with some authority.

Alf Wharmby was just about to add a clout of his own, when he noticed Sid Perkins watching him. The slimy creep would certainly report him to Pokey, so Alf changed his mind and sat down again.

Hector Bates, a deputy, spoke next: "It's nearly midnight, December twenty-third; Christmas Eve in a minute and we've very little chance of seeing Christmas Day if we don't get through in the next twelve hours. The only reason the water's not filled up already is because the air pressure is holding it back. What happens when we break through? Do we let the water in?"

"Well, we'll have to chance it, won't we?" Burgin jumped in like a shot. "If your theory's right and we're living in a giant bubble, well, it'll be a gas bubble soon and that's all of us finished. What're we going to do, sit and wait for it?"

"What if we break through and the roof's down all the way to Pinkstone?" Bert Honey's mind naturally went to food. "We could have plenty of air then, but we'd just starve to death."

"What, if we're already dead?" Philip Burgin mocked them, "This palaver is finished as far as I'm concerned." He took up a pick and went back to work by the light of the failing lamp. He was joined by two others and the work went on.

They fell back from the wall now when they had done their stint, and lay gasping almost under the legs of the next diggers. Every blow with the pick was a full blooded effort of will-power. Every shovel full of rubble was thrown as if the man had thrown a year off his life with it. Several of them vomited as they worked, the stomach muscles having given up their protective roll, leaving the unguarded intestines to take the shock and strain of bending and straightening. The vile smell they generated had crept on them gradually and was not too noticeable. The hours went on.

Fatigue was extreme now with some of them, and they refused to tunnel any further. Cliff Prentice spoke up from his coal-blackened throat. "What time is it?"

"Five-and-twenty past eight," a voice came from the back.

How the hell does he know, thought Prentice, for the lights had given out altogether now. Nevertheless they all believed him.

"It's Christmas Eve breakfast time," Bert Honey gasped. "We always have stewed leg meat for breakfast on Christmas Eve. Plenty of fresh bread with real butter on it. Mustard on the side. Nothing like stewing meat for putting stars on the bloody watter. Gravy; that thick you can chew it afore you swallow it."

"You're a gutsy swine, Honey," Alf Wharmby accused him. He was a man who liked food himself, but he could never eat his dinner while children looked on hungrily. It was common knowledge that Honey could.

"Quiet, everybody," Philip Burgin called. He stopped the men tunnelling as he did about every half hour, then he thumped on the tunnel's leading face with his pick head and listened. He could tell if they were getting near to the old Pinkstone workings by the sound, but it was still solid. They were never going to make it. He pressed his ear to the wall in the forlorn hope that he might hear Jobey coming towards them. All bitterness forgotten now. Jobey had been quietly uppermost in all their minds. With the way Booker and Waverley had needed him this past year, the way he had stamped his quiet authority on the pit and all that surrounded it – there was a kind of omnipotence about him. They had put him down as a winner.

And Norman Booker, although he was an Owner's man, born and bred, still they could trust him to move heaven and earth to help them. It looked like outside help or nothing if they didn't ... Burgin pulled his hand from the wall. It was wet and cold. Wet! He put his hands down at the bottom of the wall. Water was seeping through. God Almighty, the thin seam must be flooded. They were at the bottom of a pit with water all around and above them, hanging on to a small thread of life in a pocket of foul air, which could not support life for very much longer. Perhaps one good blow with the pick would bring the water in, and have done with it. Should he say nothing? Had he the right?

He just made his announcement: "There'll be no more digging, lads."

The silence suddenly became heavy with question and answer. The dark empty air was suddenly filled with fear and unspoken dread.

No-one asked him why, they didn't want to hear the actual pronouncement of a death sentence. He knew the terror which must have crept into their souls. Better not to hear the words spoken whatever they were. That left some tiny place at the back of the mind in which to hide. Pokey, however, had no need to hide, he had nothing of value to lose, and it showed.

"What do you mean there'll be no more bleeding digging?" He was with them again. Trampling on everybody's feelings. The Bulldog had better keep quiet too. Pokey was already feeling his way around trying to find him. Sid Perkins told him what happened.

Philip Burgin decided it might as well be said. "There's water on the other side of this wall. The thin seam is flooded."

He left them to draw their own conclusions, which they did, in the frightful claustrophobic gaseous black hole where their emotions were now stripped bare. The gut-gripping hand of stark terror reached out to them all.

As if by common consent they gathered closely together, and rough hard hands came in contact and held on. Unashamedly, they offered themselves to each other with an innocence they had withheld since childhood.

The Bulldog started a hymn, "Nearer my God to Thee" and it was taken up by them all. Midway through the last verse there was a tremendous crack from the roof, as the Doctor and Jobey blasted to try to gain time. Knowing there was not much chance now, they had resorted to laying charges and blasting through. The men knew nothing of this, and thought the roof was about to give way and let in the water. Their voices were snatched out of the air by the crack from the roof, it seemed to split their very nerve-endings and the hymn was not started again.

Cliff Prentice thought any conversation was better than none. "I had a cousin escaped from that disaster at Strelley pit, you know. He told me things that'd make your hair stand on end – but they got out of it for all that."

"Well go on then," A tremulous voice came back. Conversation made things appear normal. It got them through another few minutes, while whatever was going to happen came a little nearer.

"This was about two women fighting. The bodies had all been identified and claimed, what they had brought up, that is. Most of them was left down there, you know. The pit was sealed and a service was held for them all."

"They'll seal this one and all, before long. Lay wreaths on

top like a bloody cenotaph."

"It's sealed itself, this bugger has."

Comments came from here and there.

"Do you want to hear about what these women did or not?"

There was a silence.

"Well one of these women said that this last body was her husband, see, but it was that badly burned that nobody could tell. She said she could tell by his teeth. Well, they let her take him home and she put him in the parlour. This other woman, she never said nothing, but that night she went round with her husband's whippet. It fair went mad, that dog did. Jumped up and nearly had him off the trestles. Well, I ask ya, what can't speak can't lie, so they just took him home without further ado. How did that dog know, eh?"

Nobody replied. Air was scarce, and widows were not a good subject just now.

Old George Keetch died quietly, just as he had always lived, being no trouble to anybody. His lungs had been heavy with coal dust for many years now and were just not up to the job. Hector Bates heard the terrible noise he was making as George very slowly drowned in the putrid atmosphere. Hector made no effort to help him, the kindest thing was to let it happen and be over with. When the legs had stopped twitching Hector announced the death to the others and placed George's hands across his chest. He found a lucky bean tightly clenched in one hand. George always carried it down the pit to keep him safe.

"Are you going to say a few words over him, Oliver?" Hector asked the Bulldog.

"That I will. That I will. Where is he?"

"Right next to me, here. I've crossed his arms."

Everyone tried to breathe a little more quietly. George Keetch had been a gentle likeable soul.

The Bulldog cleared his throat in his unmistakable manner, which amounted to a call for silence.

"Ōh Ḹord, we ask Thee to accept the soul of this our brother Keetch. Let him dwell in Thy ..."

Thwack!!! "Got the bastard." The silence was shattered rudely and abruptly. It was Pokey, ratting with his shovel while the service went on.

"Accept his soul we pray Thee oh Lord, and in Thy infinite goodness and mercy ..."

Thwack! Pokey struck again. "Go steady with that shovel, Pokey." Sid Perkins moaned.

"Charming. Bloody delightful," the Bulldog said. "Have you no respect for the dead?"

Alf Wharmby could contain himself no longer. He had been a good friend of George Keetch.

"Shut your mouth, Pokey Jordan. You're not God, even if you think you are. In fact you're not a very good human, if you ask me."

Pokey was on him in a flash. He took Alf's head in his hands. "No bugger's asking you, are they?" He thumped the head hard against the floor with every word by way of emphasis.

They all had splitting headaches in the nitrogen-laden air, and to hear Alf's head being savagely thumped was a terrible thing, but no-one went to his aid. The thought of getting into Pokey's clutches in the solid blackness was not pleasant. At this moment Pokey *was* God. There was no law save that of brute force. The primitive savagery of his animal strength, and his complete lack of morals was frightening.

It seemed to them the last unendurable straw, that their predicament should be made worse by the vile beastiality of Pokey. It seemed to deny decency and dignity to the very act of dying.

"What have we done to deserve this?" An anonymous voice came out of the dark. "We've spent all year squabbling amongst ourselves, who else can we fight? God help our poor children, who've nothing to turn to for their bread except this bloody awful pit. God help *them* I say, because it's too late now for us."

There was a silence now as they contemplated their situation.

Eventually Pokey's voice came again. "Christ, what I'd do for a quarten of ale."

A deeper silence settled as some of the men began to relax their hold on life.

They were in great difficulties now, and one was crying audibly with no attempt to disguise the fact. Alf Wharmby spoke in a tight, strained voice. "I'm no bloody hero." It seemed such a right thing to say, it raised an odd chuckle here and there. Then there was a long silence as the men prepared themselves to die.

Not with any ceremony or ritual; each man must come to terms with the decision for himself. It had to involve his family, his finances, his private possessions, but most of all it concerned his immediate future, with flesh-tearing pain or lung-bursting slow agony, or some other even more unimaginable terror.

Matty Wilson looked up to where stood the trees he had loved so well, they stood now in the cool fresh air, not so very far above him. He could almost feel their rough friendly bark. The trees were solid and enduring, they would be there tomorrow and the next Christmas, his lovely trees.

And yet somehow the silent trees were not his friends any more. They pushed down at him now with their solid weight, and denounced him as being not one of them. What had he to do with living things, when he was already dead and buried? He had no tomorrow, and would not be going back amongst them. He wept for himself. He put his old cap on his knees and sobbed into it with heart-breaking shuddering sighs. God, this was awful.

No-one spoke. Words were no longer important. They were just birds, keeping in touch by sound. The intricacies of a vocabulary had been sloughed off, along with millions of years of evolutionary progress. A defence mechanism was at work which dulled the finer instincts, sound, touch, and hearing were nothing more than just that. As the silence settled, each man hoped he was not going to be the last one to die. That would be awful. That could set a man's heart pounding, just thinking about it.

Philip Burgin wondered if he ought to make an effort of some sort. They had acknowledged his leadership so far. No, to hell with it. He could lead them to life, but not to death. That was the Bulldog's job. He was being very quiet, what ailed him? Never a man to miss the chance to pontificate, this situation was tailor-made for his private disclosures of the Lord's intentions. A sudden suspicion crossed his mind.

"Where's Oliver Purdy?" The air seemed so rank the words

did not carry. He called again, as loudly as he could.

"Where's the Bulldog?"

A murmur went up, but no reply came from the foul blackness.

"Pokey. Pokey Jordan," Burgin called again.

"Shut your bleedin' mouth, Burgin. We've stopped digging. Nobody wants to hear you now," Pokey called from some distance away. Burgin crawled in the direction of the voice. Every movement measured and laborious like a climber near the peak of Everest. He found him at last.

"Pokey! What have you done with the Bulldog?" Burgin's voice was alive with his suspicions.

Pokey felt around in the darkness, but Burgin sensed the movement and drew back slightly. There was a low deep-throated chuckle from Pokey's hard barrel of a chest. He was indestructible, this hard-roaned granite-like mass of bone and muscle.

"He ran out of air." He chuckled again, and Sid Perkins echoed him dutifully.

"You killed him!" Burgin uttered the words incredulously. "You killed the Bulldog in cold blood, you bastard." He sensed the movement just before a pair of steel-like arms enclosed him.

"You're next Burgin. Good bleedin' air being wasted on you."

Burgin brought up his knee into Pokey's crutch and the pain of it almost made Pokey release his hold, but he held on until the pain subsided. Burgin lay there under Pokey's great evil-smelling body as if trapped under a horse. He knew he was on the brink of death. He felt like a fly waiting for the spider to kill. Had the shortage of oxygen affected Pokey's brain? Did Pokey intend to kill them all, one by one in the foetid blackness, to conserve the air? Were they all just so many ponies to him, 'sucking in great dollops of air'?

He began to lose consciousness. Is this what life had all been about, to leave a collection of bones six hundred feet below ground? What had this to do with the real purpose of living, with spring in Watnall Woods, and the kite-flying air over Misk Hills?

This place would be sealed, it could become a shrine. A

merciful curtain would be drawn forever over the scrabbling sordid truth. The raw stuff of self-preservation which had erupted in Pokey had stirred a base chord in many of them. They were like Butcher Barnsdall's cows after the first blow of the axe ... not seeing, not thinking. Knowing only by some deep instinct that the dreaded longed-for gift of oblivion must soon follow.

There was an almighty explosion, and pieces of the roof came in at various points. Sid Perkins took a great lump of rock onto his chest, which smashed his rib cage and pressed out what little air there was left in his body. Pokey had lost his lodger at last.

Philip Burgin just managed to gasp! "Jobey!" before he passed out.

Pokey released his hold. Jobey Rainbow? It couldn't be. The noise was a little way above them. There was no way in from there. Suddenly one of the deputies remembered Billy Musson's colliery, the little outfit that John Waverley had closed down.

"They're coming through Billy Musson's old pit," he shouted, the effort bringing on a pain in his chest. They all lay there looking at the roof. Some of the props had given way under the strain, but they had no strength left to do anything about it, except to pray. The ends of some of the props were splayed out like shaving brushes, and they knew the pressure on the roof must be enormous. Some of them were going to get buried, but some would live. There was hope. The magnificent Jobey was coming.

It was noon on December the twenty-fourth, and the crowd round the small pit at the top of Billy Musson's old shaft was about five hundred strong. Every family who had a man below ground had representatives to rush any news back to the household. Norman Booker passed on reports, and the tension grew as it became time for the break-through.

At two p.m. Jobey was through. Their roof fell in below him, and he looked down to where it fell, but could not see or know that Alf Wharmby was underneath, hands together in prayer giving thanks for their deliverance. Alf died alongside Sweetie.

The air came out of the tunnel and up the shaft past Jobey

like a jet stream. Air so foul that Jobey thought he must pass out before it had released its pressure. He turned away from it and took shallow breaths to minimise the effect.

As soon as the pressure inside had dropped, Jobey lowered himself into the workings, and found himself ankle deep in water. Leaving the following rescuers to deal with other matters, he made a quick reconnaisance trip and saw the source of the water. He picked up a now useless air door and wedged it against the abandoned tunnel which led to the Pinkstone workings. It was no use. Now the wall was down, the water was breaking through like a mill race. The water was also rising quickly from the switchback section.

"Quick, more doors here," roared Jobey. "We shan't save ourselves, never mind anybody else."

The water was now up to their knees. Four doors were jammed into the tunnel, and Jobey put his back against them. Spragging against protruding rocks on each side, he pushed backwards to hold the water if he could. It worked for a short time while the miners were roped up the rescue shaft, but the water was now up to their waists. Doctor Alexander gave the signal to abandon any further rescue attempts; all they were finding were dead bodies, and he was afraid for the safety of his own men.

One by one they got back up the emergency shaft, Dr. Alexander waiting at the bottom for Jobey. He knew Jobey had a tiger by the tail and might need some help.

"Come on now," he bellowed. Jobey released the pressure he had been exerting against the doors and the water catapulted him forward with frightening force. Jobey's muscles had stiffened in the cold water and his movements were nightmarishly slow. He looked up into the small circle of light where Dr. Alexander, spragged in the bottom of the shaft, was peering down anxiously into the writhing black tunnel of water.

Jobey came along with the water. Putting up his hands he held on to the edge of the chimney-like shaft, while the irresistible pull clutched ever harder at his body. His clothes ballooned out and pulled at him like an anchor going down. His body was horizontal to the shaft which was now full to the roof, and his head was under water.

The Doctor could see the powerful hands fastened limpet-like to the rock, the whipcord veins standing out with the strain. The water made greasy globules all over the skin, reminding him of a great bronze statue he had once seen, of Hercules wrestling with a Hydra. He reached down from his precarious hold and touched the hands. They were as cold and hard as ice. He had thought of being able to help Jobey by taking hold of his hands, but the very touch of them had been enough to convince him that he had better keep out of it! His own hands were soft and warm and vulnerable, they had led a very protected life. Jobey's were like steel. They had got to finish the job for him which they had started. He was so near now, this was the last thing they would be called upon to do in the entire rescue.

"Come on hands," he said aloud. He was willing Jobey out of the water with such intensity that he had spoken the words quite naturally.

"Margaret will be waiting, Jobey. Try a little harder son, oh try, Jobey, think of Margaret. Pull now for her sake."

Jobey shook his head and water flew in all directions. He looked further up the shaft for hand holds, and clutched a protruding piece of rock. The Doctor nodded, and again put his own hands on Jobey's, after all he had said to himself – but it was a contact of a sort. Jobey would pick up the solicitude, it must help.

There was a final contraction of those magnificent muscles, and Jobey was out clear of the death-dealing black menace. They both looked down, and even Jobey gave a shudder.

Dr. Alex took one of the hands now it was free, squeezed it in his own and rubbed a little warmth into it.

"Up you go, Jobey. Get up there where your friends are waiting."

The mention of friends lit up Jobey's whole face. He was returning to a world he had not known for a long time – it didn't take a lot to keep him happy.

A hand brushed lightly against Jobey's, paused, and withdrew; he had a vague pleasurable impression that, as once before, Minnie Varley had communicated with him, but he could not distinguish her in the crowd swirling around his weary monumental body.

Pokey was the first of the rescued to go up the shaft, naturally. He pulled himself out at the top to a very subdued cheer; if they had been betting on who would be the first man out, Pokey would have been a red hot favourite. He refused to move until the last man was out, taking a swig now and again at the quarter bottle of brandy he had been given.

Someone was taking names, and Pokey looked down the list.

"Burgin not among them?" he asked.

"No. I am dreadfully sorry." The man looked troubled.

Pokey shrugged. "Too bad." He finished the brandy and dropped the bottle down the shaft. "Here you are lads, have one on me." He chuckled at his joke as he was bundled into blankets and packed off with the others.

* * *

Booker arrived home to find Mildred waiting for him. They had seen good and bad times together, and her love was a great unspoken support for him. The walls of the familiar room enclosed him, and he took the hot sweet tea she had ready.

She put her hand into his and he was instantly aware that somebody still loved him. Hell, he really was feeling sorry for himself. He drew on her goodness, her ordinary everyday normality. It soaked up the sharp nightmares he had been through. He held on tightly. Nobody was gunning for Mildred. The blandness of her existence was an antidote to the abuse to which he would be subjected. He didn't want to know about the future – sufficient unto the day. It all had to be faced, God help him, but not today.

"How bad is it Norman? That is, if you want to talk about it."

"It couldn't be much worse, dear. Over sixty men dead, including Seth Sloman. Jobey got about forty up through Billy Musson's old pit, a bloody miracle that was, and nothing less." His eyes were shining as he blew his nose. "A bloody miracle". The tears were now flowing and she knelt beside him. "Norman, it's an act of God, don't crucify yourself. The world's full of trouble, we don't have to take it all on our own shoulders."

She sought for words to comfort him – but there were none.

"It's all right Mildred. Be all right in a minute."

"It's just reaction, Norman. Let me ring the Doctor."

"On Christmas Eve?"

"Well it's only afternoon. I mean, he won't be drunk for some time yet."

She started the process of talking him out of a state of near shock. They had a long uphill road from here, to get back to normal living.

"Where's Margaret?" He looked round.

"She's in the front room with Ralph Waverley."

He pulled a face.

"What's the matter?" she asked, then paused. "Have we been thrown to the wolves?"

He gave a sad smile, then drew a finger across his throat. He daren't trust himself with words just for the moment.

"Drink your tea, dear." She patted his hand.

He nodded towards the front room. "What does *he* want?"

Mildred hesitated, looking hard at her husband.

"John Waverley's had a heart attack."

He dropped his head and studied his feet. "Lucky bastard."

"Norman!" Her own tears were showing.

"It's no use, Mildred. I'm on my knees. You'll have to give me time."

"You're tired, darling. How long is it since you had any sleep?"

"Must be about three years." He cleared his throat. "Is Waverley dead?" His tone was flat, he may as well have asked if the kettle was boiling.

She looked at him, saying nothing.

"Oh well." His voice picked up strength. "One down to our side as well, eh?"

The door opened and Ralph Waverley came in. Margaret saw her father, and ran across the room.

"Dad! How long have you been here?"

He couldn't speak, it was obvious he was holding himself up by sheer willpower.

She took his hands and kissed them. "You're home now, Dad. Out of harm's way."

He held on to her wrist – there was no watch. He looked at her quickly, then at Ralph Waverley. Waverley had the watch in his hand, and put it on the sideboard. He spoke to Mildred: "Well it's no use to me, is it?"

The ticking of the grandfather clock took over for a minute. The world of coal outside had taken its boots off, ready for Christmas. It was almost dark already.

"Sorry about your father, Ralph." Booker found his voice at last.

"Thank you. Thank you, Norman." Young Waverley had been cloned out of pure mine owner's stock. Tall, slim; well-modulated voice, not a trace of local accent.

"We'll have to have a talk very soon, Norman. I mean, these Union Johnnies could be making a meal out of this. They'll want to rewrite the rule books. Holidays with pay, early retirement. They'll want their own men on the Board, next." He looked fierce just for a moment. "My father would be alive now if he had ..." He stopped suddenly.

Booker said nothing. His father had told him, years ago, 'You learn to love while you're loving, Norman. You learn to hate while you're hating.' He had done all the hating he was going to do. Nineteen twenty-six had seen its share of confrontation, it had been a bad year for all who lived by coal; sometime the hating had to stop.

"Well," Ralph Waverley pulled on his gloves. "It hardly seems appropriate, but I wish you all a Merry Christmas. We'll let the New Year take care of itself – what?"

"Merry Christmas, Ralph", they all returned. Then he was gone.

Booker fished into a cupboard for whisky. "He'll be back."

Margaret shook her head. "No", she looked through the window into the gathering gloom, "No, he won't."

Father and daughter looked at one another, cautiously, hopefully.

"It's Jobey is it?" Booker asked.

Margaret nodded, and sneaked a look at her Mother. "Yes," she said, "and to hell with Aunt Beatrice."

Booker held up his glass: "To hell with our Beatrice."

Mildred picked up her drink: "It's *your* sister." She raised the glass. "Whatever you say, dear." She caught his eye. "You know, there's nothing wrong with this family that a couple of grandchildren couldn't cure."

Margaret put on her coat, still looking through the window.

"Is he there?" Mildred asked.

"Who?" Margaret turned, then smiled. "Yes, he's in the lane now, doing his great bear act as if nothing had happened."

"Then bring him in, dear." Mildred brought out another glass. "Christmas is a time for miracles. I reckon he's just what this family needs – and who's going to argue with us, if we've got Jobey on our side."

She held up her glass: "You toast the New Year dear, if Ralph Waverley daren't." She lowered her voice. "Whatever it brings, eh Norman?"

He nodded, almost asleep. Too tired to think, he raised his glass and gave the stock phrase they all used at the pit – God rest Tater's soul: "There be Dragons."

She looked at him with a determined jaw.

"And who's afraid of Dragons?"

Margaret went to her Mother and with a great surge of love, kissed her, blinking back her tears.

" 'Cos we've got Jobey Rainbow."

"Warts and all," said Mildred, and downed the whisky.